Jubilee

NEPI SOLOMON

TANDEM PRESS

First published in 1994
New edition 2000 by
TANDEM PRESS
2 Rugby Road, Birkenhead, Auckland 10
New Zealand

Copyright © 1994 text Nepi Solomon
ISBN 1-877178-66-7

Cover: Magma Design
Typesetting: Graeme Leather
Photographs by Glenn Jowitt, copyright © South Pacific Pictures
Printed in Australia by Australian Print Group

One

Billy Williams piled hot fries onto a slab of white bread then slopped on the tomato sauce before folding the lot into a chunky wad. Biting into it, he was flooded by a moment of pure bliss. He swallowed and said, 'It only happens once every twenty-five years. A Jubilee, that is.'

It was Sunday lunchtime. Everybody except Billy's wife, Pauline, was dipping into a heap of fish and chips that was spread in its wrapping paper on the table.

She just stared at him. Her face was as white as the fish-shop paper and she had that hard look in her eyes.

Billy said, 'We had the seventy-fifth last time, so now it's the hundredth.'

'You don't say.' Fourteen-year-old Lucille reached for the sauce bottle. She made a clearing and squirted a puddle of tomato sauce onto the paper.

'Those cheeky buggers on the committee said I'll never make the next one, the way I'm going, so they said I have to be the chairman!'

'And you agreed? Oh, Billy!' Pauline got up from the table and stood at the sink, looking out through a window that was grey with wavy rain patterns.

Her gesture annoyed Billy; whenever there was a disagreement she walked away, as if underlining the difference between herself and Billy's family. Billy's mother reckoned that all pakeha were the same, that none of them would stand their ground and talk things out in the civilised Maori way.

He appealed to his wife: 'Hey . . . don't be like that. Come and sit down, eh.'

'But Billy, you promised.'

Through the rain she could see lots of other promises: a tank-stand that needed painting, a fence waiting to be fixed, a patchy blue and brown Mark Three Zephyr that was towed here almost good as new nearly two years ago, a wilderness of weeds that was a thriving vegie garden before she started that job in Te Kuiti and Billy agreed to take it over, and remnants of a load of firewood delivered last winter and never stacked away under the tank-stand on account of the junk already there. Beyond, a bedraggled hen in a nest of weeds, was the original Williams place. That eyesore was supposed to've been pulled down years ago.

Lucille stopped chewing and watched her parents.

Billy felt a flare of anger. Pauline could at least try to be reasonable. Did she really expect him to turn his back on the district? He was born and raised right here, never strayed more than a hundred kilometres in any direction. The district was *him*, his blood, his life.

'Look, I owe them — okay?' And when her back stayed rigid: 'It's a fucking compliment, for heaven's sake! I'm going to be the Master of Ceremonies too. It's the best job of the lot. I get to run things — make all the announcements, tell all the jokes . . . '

'You said you wouldn't get conned into anything else. Not after that sports pageant.'

'Conned! It's no such — '

'You dumped on us last time, Billy Williams. Don't you forget that. Besides, you got no free time as it is. Not with coaching the juniors.'

Young Thomas reached across and thieved Lucille's second piece of fish. He dragged it through the puddle of sauce and was about to cram it into his mouth when she saw him.

'Mum! Look what the little sod's doing!'

Billy cuffed his son. Thomas yelled, but stopped the moment his father raised his hand again. Lucille took her fish fillet back and picked off the part that her brother had touched.

Shoulders slumped, Pauline stared through the rain at the Zephyr. It was going to be fixed up for her. Their second car, Billy promised. She could still see the eager look on his face when it arrived, towed behind his double-cab ute. It was supposed to be hers, so's she didn't have to get up so early to catch the bus to work. So's she didn't have to stand in the rain getting her shoes soaked, and wait on frosty mornings with her arse freezing off. Now it was coming into winter again. The car looked dead. Long green needles of kikuyu grass poked out around the bonnet.

Auntie Minnie tried to cheer things up. She was so fat that she wheezed when she spoke. 'Hey you fullahs, eat up. Come on, Paulie. Potu bought your favourite. Paua fritters. They's getting cold.'

'They's getting eaten by the locust.' From Lucille.

Now Billy got up from the table. He put an arm around his wife. He smiled at her. He still looked just like Cliff Richard when he smiled.

'That's the way, you two. Kiss and make up,' said Minnie.

'You promised.' Pauline was angry now. 'You said you wouldn't do one more damned thing for that bloody school committee until everything around here was tidy.'

Uneasy, Potu pushed his chair away from the table. He was a nervous little man with round eyes like a bird's. He wiped his greasy fingers on the newspaper wrappings. 'See you fullahs later, okay? Come on, Minnie. Move that fat bum of yours. We'se going home.'

'Speak for yourself.' She slapped his hand when he nudged her.

Billy pretended surprise at his wife's outburst. 'Is that all that's twisting your tits? Just a few jobs around here? They'll get done, no sweat. I promise.'

'Yes, you promise. You can do that all right.' Then Pauline began to laugh. 'You promise? You *promise?*' She laughed and laughed.

Relieved, Potu sat down again. Once Pauline started to laugh it was a sign everything was okay. He peeled another slice off the cut loaf and hooked his finger into the margarine container, towing it close. He hated quarrels, especially when it was his brother and his wife. 'That's the way, Paulie. Hoe in, eh. There's a couple a' oysters somewhere there, too, if that rascal of yours hasn't scoffed them.'

Billy shook Potu's empty beer can. 'How about another round? There's a dozen Lion Red in the fridge.'

'I'll try to force them down, eh,' Potu grinned.

'There's DB but it's warm.'

'Lion'll do.' Potu was never fussy if someone else was shouting.

'And you ladies?'

Minnie said, 'Us ladies'll have Jim Beam and Coke. Okay Paulie?'

'There's only L and P left,' accused Lucille. 'Bet you can't guess where all the Coke went.'

Billy ruffled his son's hair. He was feeling great. It had gone off well, considering, he thought as he piled more soggy chips on to another piece of bread. That was round one to him, until she found out that he'd also volunteered to help Bobo Penny with the secretarial work. The shit would really hit the fan when that came out.

Aaah, no sweat, he thought. He'd think of something to smooth her down. She was okay, was Paulie.

After school next day Lucille sat on the back steps chucking scraps of bread to her pet chooks while Auntie Minnie sat on the step above her, brushing her hair. She ripped the bread up into tiny bits so's it would last longer.

There were three chooks left from the eight day-old chicks Granny had sent up from Nefta's place on the bus. The seven dwarfs and Snow White, peeping fluff in a shoe-box with holes punched in the top.

The cat dealt with three of them, and two had died early on, but these three looked like surviving, providing they were hens. Billy wasn't about to have some bloody rooster telling him it was morning at three a.m. when he'd been on the skoot the night before. No way.

'They're all girls, aren't they?' Lucille asked Minnie as Grumpy, Doc and Dopey darted at the crumbs. They had soft, reddish feathers and inquisitive eyes.

Minnie dragged the brush through Lucille's hair. It was almost a metre long and the colour of shiny toffee. 'Mmm, I dunnow. That one with the specks on its back, its comb looks as if it's getting bigger to me. Whaddaya reckon?'

Lucille shivered. Doc was her favourite.

Minnie understood. 'Aaah, yer dad won't chop him.'

'He reckoned he would.'

Minnie shrugged. She lit up a Winfield Blue and puffed smoke rings over Lucille's head.

Lucille leaned against Aunt Minnie's cushiony thighs and watched the smoke rings float by. The air was so still that she could poke her forefinger through each one before it dissolved. It was a prime spot here, looking clear along the valley.

The hills were an autumn gold, all creased across where thousands of sheep over many decades had crimped the slopes into ridges. Orange and yellow fruit trees clustered around farmhouse roofs, set back off the road away from the dust and traffic, not that there was much of that now that the timber mill had shut down. Killed the valley when that went, everyone said, though the district still looked pretty much alive to Lucille. Native bush bristled thick along the river flat. Tuis and bellbirds and lots of insects lived there.

Minnie pinched out her cigarette. 'French plait again, eh? Maybe I can do it like that for the Jubilee dance. You'll look fan-bloody-tastic.'

'I probably won't even go.'

'*Everybody* will go. I remember the last one. Whooee! I was only about seven, but what a party!' She lapsed into silence, thinking that if she wanted to fit into any of her old ball gowns she'd have to lose at least twenty kilos. Ah, the hell with it, she thought as she punched Lucille's shoulder.

'I'm one of the olds now, but you . . . You's old enough to really get into it. Dance the night away, hey?'

'Nobody'll dance with me.'

'No boyfriend yet?'

'Don't want one. All the boys at High School are *gross.*'

Minnie laughed. She sounded like someone squeezing a leaky balloon. 'Tell you what, kiddo. Grown-

8

up men are even worse. They just get more cunning — they hide it better.'

Lucille doubted that. She had her eye on someone who had left school. Felipe Watene. *He* wasn't gross. Most afternoons he and his brother Denis were lounging about on the benches in the Domain near where she caught the bus home. They wore leathers and smoked, and were too important to notice a plain little nobody in a school uniform.

Lucille thought about Felipe while Minnie divided her hair into sections. The chooks came back and pecked at her sandals, hinting. Someone had lit a rubbish fire, way in the distance, down past the Taki place. The smoke formed in a ball at the base, then teased into a strand going straight up into the sky. Like soft new wool being spun, thought Lucille.

She was about to say how lovely the valley was on an afternoon like this, when Minnie spoke.

'Shit but it's quiet. Gives me the creeps when it's like this . . . It seems like there's gonna be an earthquake any minute, or a bomb gonna drop.' She shuddered.

Against her back, Lucille could feel Minnie's body wobbling. It was a bit like an earthquake itself.

Two

Because nothing much ever happened in Waimatua (pop. 274 at last census), when something *did* come up everybody wanted to get in on the act. In the beginning, that is. When the plans were being laid. When there was a lot of talking and not much doing. Everyone wanted to feel important then.

They were great at rallying round at the end, too. Say what you like, but even Pauline admitted that when it came to putting down a hangi or baking fifty cream sponges or whipping up piu piu and headbands for a concert team, there was nobody to match the citizens of Waimatua. Their community spirit would leave any city suburb for dead.

No, it was in the middle bit that they wilted. When the boring stuff needed doing. The real work. Writing letters. Making lists. Painting posters. Scrounging for sponsorship. Organising. That's when the good keen citizens disappeared like rats under the old Williams place.

That's when the excuses could fill an encyclopaedia, Pauline reckoned.

And, she said, that's when Mr Muggins ended up with the whole bloody lot in his lap. Which meant her lap too. Hers and Lucille's and Minnie's. And she wasn't half sick of it.

'Hey, are y' coming to the meeting?' Billy was slicked down and spruced up, looking his Cliff Richard best. Faded but still smooth.

'No thanks.' Pauline sat at the kitchen table, drinking tea. Thomas and Lucille sat opposite, toying with their homework.

'Aw, come on. The Crawfords will be there. And the Morrisons.'

Big deal, she thought, but said nothing.

'When you hear a bit about the Jubilee you'll be as keen as the rest of them, you'll see.'

'I'll hear enough about it pretty soon.' She tossed the dregs down the sink and rinsed the mug.

'Mum, how do you spell "insecticide"?'

'Where's your dictionary?'

'Left it at school. Lucille won't lend me hers.'

'D'ya blame me?'

'Lucille — '

'Oh, all right.' She nudged it across the red formica and as soon as he touched it she rounded on her brother. 'And no more scribbling in it, *if* you don't mind!'

'Scribbling?' As a rule Billy tried to keep out of their quarrels, a policy which caused more quarrels between him and Pauline. He called it open responsibility. She called it fence sitting, negligent parenting and a few other things besides.

'He's put circles around all the rude words, Dad.' She snatched the dictionary back and flicked pages, showing him *fart* and *fornicate* and *fuck*. Billy was shocked. Were those words in the dictionary when he was at school?

'What'll I do if the teacher sees it?'

Thomas was cowering and defiant at the same time. He said, 'Maybe you should tear the pages out.'

'It's the school's, you spastic nerd! I have to hand it back at the end of the year. Old witch Maxwell checks them all, too.'

Billy frowned. 'You could try rubbing it out.'

'It's felt-tip, Dad. These dictionaries cost fifteen dollars each on the book list.'

Which shocked him again. Shit, fifteen dollars! Though rocked, he adopted his usual attitude. 'We'll talk about it later. Look at the time. I have to go. Hey, come on Pauline. Sure you won't change your mind?'

Pauline was setting up the sewing machine. 'I've got to finish those warm slacks before the winter starts. I froze last year, waiting for the bus.'

Billy felt doubly guilty then. Guilt irritated like acid. 'No need to keep rubbing it in.'

'Rubbing what in?'

'You know damned well.' He shifted from one foot to the other.

'Got to go.'

'Goodbye, then.' From Pauline. The children were hissing at each other but she would straighten things out when he had gone.

Nobody looked up. He stamped out to the ute and started it with a roar.

Pauline sighed as she threaded the needle. There was nothing like being in the wrong for putting Billy in a mood.

An hour later his mood was no better. The committee, plus all the district, it seemed, were jammed into the old school building, a musty, creaky hall, designed with windows set high so that children couldn't see out and, therefore, had to concentrate on their school work. There was a smart new two-roomed block now, with floor-to-ceiling windows in the modern style, but in their time Billy and Potu had attended class here. From their old two-seater desks they could see only sky. At the moment the windows couldn't be seen either, on account of a fug of tobacco smoke. The air was thick enough to stuff cushions.

'Surely we can settle this one thing,' said Billy. Rangi Kaawa, the elder of the district, had put forward a motion to restrict smoking during meetings.

'It's a damn good idea.' From Potu. 'Smoking gets fair on my wick.'

'You leave your wick out of this,' snapped Minnie. 'I'm sick of your bloody wick.'

Jim Penny said, 'Us non-smokers can catch cancer from other people's smoke, you know.'

Mary Taki said, 'Bullshit! This is the same like it gets down the pub. None of you's bloody minds it down there.'

'Telling us what to do is just another infringement of personal liberties.' From Bobo Penny, the secretary. She had a mouth like a big red plum. The saucer in front of her sprouted long butts with plum-coloured ends.

'Too bloody right!' said Minnie. 'You fullahs 'spects us to work like bleeding slaves, but first thing you's do is interfere with our liberties and try and lay down the law, eh.'

Rangi Kaawa stood up slowly. Raising a hand for silence, he tried to speak, but coughed. He was the most respected man in the district and was tall and distinguished with a pure-white thistle-fluff of hair. He also suffered from asthma.

His coughing sounded ugly and desperate. The room gradually went quiet. Everybody watched him as he hunched his shoulders inside the red tartan rug he wore over his clothes. The noise seemed to go on and on and on. Everybody who had defended their rights to smoke began to look embarrassed. Minnie shoved her cigs and lighter into her skirt pocket.

Finally Kevin Crawford, the headmaster, spoke. He was a tall, beaky man who always reminded Billy of a wading bird. 'I'm sure that nobody wants to lay down the law, but nobody wants to cause others to suffer, either. Perhaps we can reach an acceptable compromise. If those who wish to smoke could just step outside during a meeting whenever the need moves them, then nobody's rights would be infringed.'

Billy looked at Mr Crawford as if he was the Three Wise Men rolled into one. 'Let's have a motion on that, then. Anybody second it?'

'Good idea. That sounds fair, eh.' Minnie got in before Potu could speak. No way was he going to be able to brag about cutting her down to size.

The vote was carried unanimously. Billy rapped the tack hammer that served as his gavel. He was beginning to enjoy his job. Rangi Kaawa had stopped coughing. He looked serene. When he met Billy's gaze he winked.

The meeting fell into arguments again and again while Billy struggled to keep order. Mr Crawford saved the situation a couple more times, but then came an issue that everybody wanted to argy-bargy about: the actual location of the convention, especially the Big Do on the Saturday night.

To make things easier, Billy wrote the ideas one at a time on the big blackboard behind him, together with the name of the person who made the suggestion.

Minnie and Potu wanted to hold the whole thing at the pa at the head of the valley. Do it Maori style, they urged. Show a pride in their culture. The Jubilee could make good use of the meeting house and the marae.

Rangi Kaawa said that it was a school function, so everything should take place at the school.

'Oh, I do hope so,' breathed Mrs Crawford. 'This means so much to Kevin.'

Mary Taki wanted to hold a Grand Ball at the Regency ballroom in Te Kuiti. She suggested a hundred-years-ago theme. Bobo Penny thought that if they were going to go posh, then they could hire the Floating Palace, get it towed upriver to here and use it for a real gala evening. Fireworks and a bonfire on the riverbank would add a truly festive touch.

Awhitu Osborne stepped forward. He had put a dozen kids through the school, three of them still there, and ran the Five Hundred evenings to raise money for sports equipment every year. He demanded to know what was wrong with the Waimatua pub. It had its own functions room, everything they needed for a great evening was right there, and everyone was familiar with the place.

'Too bloody familiar, some of you!' wheezed Minnie. That raised quite a laugh. The pub was Awhitu's second home. Many said his first.

Jessie and Janey Morrison, elderly spinsters who ran a farm halfway up the valley, suggested that an evening function wasn't necessary at all. A sports afternoon followed by a hangi was all they ever had in the old days, and everyone always found that perfectly adequate. Those who wanted to stay on could sing songs around a bonfire.

Nobody pointed out that these two were harking back to a time when everyone travelled by horseback because there were no proper roads. Billy wrote down their suggestion on the blackboard along with everybody else's.

When there were no more ideas, he read them out and then asked people to put their hands up to vote for what they thought was the best.

The result was:

The marae 8 votes
The school 7 votes
The Regency 5 votes
The Floating Palace 5 votes
The picnic 3 votes
Various other schemes 1 vote
And the pub 24 votes

'Well,' said Billy, taken aback. 'I guess that settles that.'

Mr Crawford tapped his biro against his chin. 'If I might interrupt before we make this law, so to speak. There are one or two points that need to be considered. I'm sure all of us who voted for the pub would like to be there right now —' he paused for the laughter, '— but have we really thought this through? Is the pub truly the best place for a school function?'

'It's so unimaginative! My idea of the Floating Palace — '

'A grand occasion needs a grand setting. That's why I think the Regency — '

'Our picnic is a much more wholesome idea,' Janey Morrison cut in. 'Fresh air, exercise — '

'Yes, Miss Morrison. We'll no doubt be going along with your idea as well as the evening function,' soothed Billy. 'Quiet please, all of you! Mr Crawford is right. Perhaps this is something we should all think about a bit more. And we should consider the costs involved.' He gazed around the hall. A dozen minor arguments were percolating, and hardly anybody was listening to him.

'Be *quiet*!' snapped Mrs Crawford. She was a chunky woman with no neck and thick brows that gave her otherwise pleasant face a surly expression. Everybody ignored her, too.

This is hopeless! Billy thought, and suddenly had a brainwave. Rapping the tack hammer until there was a complete silence, he said, 'If all those who put forward suggestions could come along to next Thursday night's meeting armed with more information and a comprehensive breakdown of what it would cost to hire each venue, then we can go into this whole issue more thoroughly.' He rapped the tack hammer again to silence the grumbling. 'And now, if I declare this meeting closed, those of us who voted for the pub can go and check the facilities there.'

Which raised the biggest cheer of all.

Three

'Crawford's right, you know. This is no place for a school dance. You want to involve all them little snappers. Jaysus, yer can't have them innocent little darlin's running about in here, wiping their sticky little fingers over everything.' This from Michael O'Reay, the manager of the Waimatua Tavern. He was a nuggety little Irishman. Every part of his exposed skin was covered with freckles and gingery hair.

'I'd 'a thought you'd be keen to get the business.' Though Billy agreed. He'd never thought much of holding do's at the pub.

'We'll do well enough, I'm thinkin'. Accommodation, to begin with. And the wee drams folks are needin' before they go off to hear borin' speeches. An' I'll be givin' you a special rate for the kegs so you'll not be goin' to that wholesaler in Te Kuiti. Aye, we'll do well enough. Now, is it draught you'll be wantin', same as usual?' As he pulled the jug full and set it on the grating for the froth to flow away he confided, 'Jaysus, it's not a lack of customers that's my problem. It's what they be doin' that's givin' me grief.'

'Whaddaya mean?'

'What I'm meaning, is that I'm getting sick and tired of them dirty bastards who urinate against that wall o' mine, round the back there.'

'What?' said Potu and Billy together.

'Filthy buggers.'

Billy nudged Potu hard. It was his shout.

'Incredible, ain't it? Jaysus, worse'n dogs, some o' the bastards I get in here.'

'Yeah, I s'pose . . .' Potu put down the money slowly, looking at each coin in turn.

'Not you two, o'course.'

'Oh, o'course!'

'It's these passers-by. That's the trouble with being located as we are in such a prime position on the main highway. You get all the riff-raff in creation. You two know I've got a fine urinal, scrubbed out clean every day and the floor polished to shine like an angel's smile. But these passing strangers, what do they know? Jaysus! They think that country folk don't have indoor plumbing, so instead of bothering to look, they just step outside and . . . !'

'What are you talking about? You all look so serious.' Bobo had just come sashaying over to the bar.

Michael O'Reay's voice went all silky. 'It's nothing a lady would be wanting to bother her pretty head about, especially not a pretty head like yours, Mrs Penny.'

She gave him a long, long smile.

Billy was annoyed. 'Let me buy you a drink.'

Michael purred, 'Gin and tonic, right? Ice?'

'Yes please.' She was still smiling at him.

Billy whispered in her ear, 'You know what ice is . . . It's just water with a hard-on.' He put his arm around her and squeezed, so that his thumb felt one soft, full breast.

She pulled away. 'You're so funny, Billy.'

Potu whistled. Billy turned his head and saw Pauline settling at a table with Minnie. She was glaring at him. Bobo took her drink, smiled at Michael one more time, thanked him instead of Billy and went over to join the ladies. Shit, though Billy. Bobo and Pauline together. That was just what he needed.

Minnie waved, mouthing that the women wanted their usual jug of Jim Beam and Coke. Michael nodded, and got it ready. Billy dug in his pocket to pay for Bobo's drink. He had nothing smaller than a ten. Michael slapped fifty cents' change down.

'Hey — the jug's on him.'

Potu grinned. 'Next round, eh. Fix you up then.'

'You shitty bugger. Whaddaya say to a game of pool?'

'Let's have a couple a' jugs first, eh? I'm dry as a chip.'

'Nah. I feel like it now. C'mon Potu. How does five bucks a game sound?'

Potu considered. Minnie was lighting up, which reminded him that she'd give him arseholes for going against her over that smoking business. Paulie looked like thunder. Bet she'd seen Billy copping a feel of the gorgeous Bobo.

'Make it ten and you're on.'

'Come on! Five, eh?'

Potu knew when he had the upper hand. 'Ten!'

Billy groaned. One way or another, this was going to be an expensive evening.

Lucille watched her mother stir the custard. The wooden spoon carved a wake through the thick yellow goo.

'I hate custard.'

'It's your dad's favourite.'

'Why do we have to have stuff Dad likes all the time? Why — '

'Just because.'

'Did you and Dad have to get married?'

'*What?*'

'You know, like, were you pregnant? I been wondering — '

'Then you can stop wondering, thank you, young lady!'

'I mean, I want to know if I started life somewhere romantic, eh, like on a picnic by the river, or in the sand dunes with waves crashing in the distance.'

Pauline thought briefly about the old Ford car with the squeaky springs and the windows that were misted up on the inside. Billy blew on them so's nobody could see in. She cried a lot, back then, and Billy always comforted her. More and more these days she tried to remember why it had all seemed so exciting, so *important*.

She sighed. 'We pay for our mistakes in life. Remember that, young lady. Now set the table, quickly.'

'Isn't my turn!'

'Wash your hands first.'

'Oh, *Mum*!'

'Hurry now. And call your father. Dinner's ready!'

The hundred-years theme was a good one, reckoned Billy, but it was too corny. Been done to death. Besides, what were they celebrating? A hundred years of pakeha occupation, that's what. Waimatua went back a lot further than that. Maybe even a thousand years to the First Fleet.

He was sitting with the fellows at the pub next night.

'It's a school jubilee, eh? You's can't drag everything else into it,' said Awhitu Osborne. He scratched his chest through the holes in his dirty black singlet. Grey hairs sprouted through the holes.

'Why not? Think about it. We got heaps more to celebrate than a school.'

'Like what?'

'Like our history.'

'What history?'

'The mill, for one thing.'

'That's dead and gone, eh. All them fullahs did was throw half the district on the dole.'

Billy felt desperate. These were all good mates — the best — but when Billy tried to put an idea across he felt as if he was bouncing a ball against a wall. 'Listen will you! This is our chance to put our district on the map. Make the rest of New Zealand take notice.'

'Take notice of you, I s'pose.'

'Give over,' Billy glared at Potu.

'Only kidding . . . But why draw attention to this dump? People's only laugh at us.'

'I don't see why.'

'I mean, lookit us! Tinpot little place, good for nothing but swamps an' possums.'

'But what I'm saying is, we got a history. Our history goes back more than a measly hundred years. What about before, eh? When there was a pa up on the hill by Mary Taki's place. There was a tribe living there, growing kumara all around on the river flats.'

Honi Fells giggled. He was as big and blubbery as his sister Minnie. 'Dunno about that, eh? Our ancestors used to spend half their time hiding in the bush from Waikato tribes, so's them buggers they wouldn't fling us in their hangi, along with our kumara they pinched, eh.'

'Cut the crap.'

'That's no lie. Whenever the Tainui had a craving for some nice fresh meat, they used to hop on their horses, eh, an' ride through the bush here, an' . . .'

Billy was annoyed. He wanted to glorify their district, but all his mates wanted to do was take the mickey. 'Don't be as thick as you look,' he snapped, but stopped when he saw the expression on Honi's face. Shit, he'd done it now.

Not mentioning certain things was unwritten law around Waimatua. Like Potu's baldness, or Minnie's weight, or Awhitu's filthiness, you didn't call Honi thick, not if you liked your health. He'd spent five years in the primers and only left Primary School when he was too big to fit behind a desk. Maybe he couldn't spell 'nosebleed' but his head-butts would do Mike Tyson proud.

'I didn't mean nothing.'

'Like hell you didn't.' Honi got up from his chair.

'Ah, shit.' Billy left.

Rangi Kaawa was sitting by his front door, catching the last of the evening light. His was an ancient grey house with a rusty iron roof that curled like a cresting wave over the disintegrating verandah. Two tall palm trees bracketed the porch, with a clothes line strung between so's the drying socks and jerseys hung under shelter. Rangi lived in the old house with his daughter Titewhai, three of her children and Rangi's assorted great-grandchildren.

A powhiri, or formal greeting, was in order. After he had approached in a deferential manner, pressed noses and sniffed the old man on both cheeks, Billy pushed damp nappies aside, dragged a chair away from the wall and sat down facing him. 'Tell me about our district,' he said. 'Tell me again about times long ago. Pretend I am still a young tamaiti, one of your mokopuna.'

'But you are a grown man, eh. Grown men don't want to hear those old stories.'

'I do.'

Rangi sucked on his inhaler, and hitched his blanket around his shoulders. A black and white cat stirred in his lap. Its hairs were all over the red wool. He nodded. Wishing to hear was reason enough, and Rangi needed little excuse to trot out his well-honed fables of olden times.

Billy said, 'I want to be proud of our district.'

'But you are proud already. I seen you there, chairing the meeting, and I think, this man is confident of who he is.'

'Thank you, Rangi Kaawa, for that sentiment, but right now my pride is only a feeling in my guts. I want to *know*. I want that feeling in my head as well. What I want is . . . authority. Yes, authority!'

What he really wanted was weapons. A verbal head-butt to fix those shit-stirrers at the pub when they pissed on his ideas. But he knew better than to express his thoughts so crudely to Rangi Kaawa.

The old man warned, 'My stories are not of authority. They are food for the spirit.'

Billy grew impatient. 'Then my spirit is hungry, okay? So tell me your stories again.'

Rangi Kaawa smiled. 'Then make yourself comfortable, eh.'

Four

A crowing rooster woke Billy at four-thirty. He had a headache. The bloody rooster's fault. He'd make the bastard crow, all right.

Pauline had forgotten to make his lunch again. Muttering, he buttered bread and slopped jam out of a tin. He left crumbs and everything he'd used lying in a mess on the bench so's she'd know. Then, instead of letting the car roll down the drive, he let it rip with a roar outside the bedroom window.

It was fifteen minutes' drive to the bush clearing where his log-trimming machine was parked. He'd start an hour earlier and knock off an hour earlier for the next few days. That'd give him time to nip home, shower and hop over to Bobo's place. They'd get in a good couple of hours, working back through years of the school attendance records, before Pauline came home from work.

Jim was no problem. He was on middle shifts at the dairy factory for all this month.

As the car's headlights carved the way out of the darkness ahead Billy tried to remember how long it had been since Jim's shifts had been of major interest. His life had revolved around that duty roster. The recollection made him smile.

'The things the devil makes us do!' he said aloud.

If he was lucky that ol' devil might come across for him again.

Lucille tugged at the French plait then gouged at the

tangled strands with her plastic hairbrush. She could've wet herself when Felipe Watene pulled it as she walked past. He nearly jerked her off her feet. Her school books had flung all over the place.

She didn't half let him have it, either. Slammed him to the max. He was impressed. She could see that by the way he backed away, saying, 'Hey . . . hey . . . all right!'

She grinned at herself in the bathroom mirror. 'Right on, girl!'

Her French plait was a disaster though, and had been all day. Maybe that's why Felipe pulled it.

Her father barged in, startling her more than Felipe had.

'Whadda you doing here?' he said.

'What about you?'

'Haven't you got netball practice or something?'

'Doesn't start 'til next week.' She stared at him. 'Are you sick? You look funny.'

'I'm busy. I've got school committee work to do, for this Jubilee thing. Don't mention it to your mother, okay?'

Lucille shrugged and tugged the brush through the last bit of unravelled plait.

'Where's Thomas?'

'Dunno. Down at Takis', I guess.'

'Minnie about?'

'She's sewing. Got a new batch of cut-outs delivered this morning. Housecoats. Awesome designs. Hey . . . she reckons I might be able to buy one for Mum's birthday, you know, at discount rate. Doesn't reckon it would cost much, either.'

Damn. Pauline's birthday again, already. He never could remember the date until too late. 'Out you go. Gonna take a shower.'

She was peeling potatoes at the sink when he came through. 'See you later,' he said, and hurried out before she could smell the aftershave. He'd been a bit too liberal, and hoped it would wear down a bit before he reached Bobo's place.

Lucille dried her hands and scooped up her armload of books. She followed him out and down the path. The chooks came racing around the side of the house. Doc's wings were flapping like he was about to take off.

When Billy reached the road gate he saw her. 'Where the hell d'you think you're going?'

'Over to Pennys' with you.'

'Like hell you are.'

Lucille flicked back her long, long hair. It was wavy in brown, shiny patterns like ripples on a mudbank. 'Yep. I'm going to help the twins with their homework.'

'The hell you are.'

'It's a job. Brilliant, eh? Mrs Penny's paying me. They've got to read every night and she's too busy to hear them herself while all this Jubilee business is going on.'

'And whose idea was this?' Not that he needed to ask.

'Dunno. Mum told me about it this morning. Hey .. . I might be able to save enough for the housecoat.'

Billy felt savage. He picked up a stick and flung it at the chooks.

'Don't do that!'

'Bloody things. One of 'em's for the chop, soon as I work out which one's making that bloody racket in the morning.'

'They're my *pets*!'

She looked about to cry. Billy stamped across the road and down the track towards the swing bridge. The stamping cleared his head. When he was part way along he turned back. 'She's a clever woman, your mother. Don't you forget it.'

Minnie and Paulie were stuffing and sealing envelopes while they watched a repeat of *Miami Vice*. Pauline missed this episode first time round, so she was trying to follow the story. This looked like a good one — for once it didn't seem to be about drugs. The story also took her mind off the annoyance that, as she predicted, already she was having this Jubilee stuff dumped on her.

Billy couldn't do it of course; he was taking a spot of pre-season tackling practice outside under the porch lights with Thomas and the others from the Under Seven Stone side. They were all shouting at once. Lucille's radio was blasting away in her room, and every time Don Johnson went off-camera Minnie started blathering about the races on Saturday. Don Johnson loomed into close-up. Minnie lit up a cigarette. 'Whew! He could give me stubble-rash any time! What about an all-over scrape-down from him, eh?'

'What would Uncle Potu say if he caught you?' From Lucille in the doorway.

'You's shouldn't be listening.'

'Go on . . . If he caught you with Don Johnson, what would he say?'

'Aaah. He'd reckon it was about time he had a night off for once.'

For once? Lucille was astonished. That meant they did it every day. Far out! she couldn't even *picture* it! Huge Auntie Minnie and little Uncle Potu. How could they fit it together? Even if his thingy was three times longer than normal (six inches was the average length of the male penis, according to Miss Pring in hygiene class), that stomach of hers would make it impossible for him to get close enough to her doings to poke it in.

'A night off?'

Minnie's giggles sounded like balloons being scrunched. High and squeaky. 'Naaah! If Potu found me tossing the sheets with Don Johnson he would ask for his autograph then bugger off to the pub to earn a bit of money betting that nobody could guess who I was screwin'.'

'Minnie!'

'Aaah, sorry, Paulie. But I betya she hears worse than that at school every day of the week.'

'Much worse, Mum. Honest.'

'That's not the point.'

'This is *mild*. Honest.'

Minnie was unrepentant. 'It's life, eh?' Don Johnson's face spread over the screen again and she sighed hugely. 'Not my life, though. But lucky for some.' She giggled again. 'Makes your mouth water, eh? No sweat licking envelopes with him on the box!'

Pauline still looked prim. 'Finished your homework, Lucille?'

'I'm getting heaps done at Pennys' — my project of the Amazon rainforest is almost finished.'

'See what I mean?' said Pauline. 'They teach them all about the Amazon rainforests and half of them can't recognise the trees in our own native bush.'

'Give over, Mum.'

'Well, it's true. Remember that barbecue, when your friends came out from town?'

Lucille remembered being mortified to the max. Afterwards Rima said sarcastically, 'Your mother's the whitest Maori I ever seen.'

'They could identify a kauri, a rimu and a totara, and that was it! Why? Because nobody had ever bothered to teach them, that's why! No wonder we're losing our culture! I've half a mind to go up to the high school and tell that principal of yours what I think.'

'Why don'tcha, then?' Lucille acted uninterested, though she'd've died if her mother actually did show up. She picked a folded paper out of the stack and opened it. The commercials were on now, so she read it aloud:

' "ONE HUNDRED YEARS!
THE WAIMATUA SCHOOL PROUDLY
CELEBRATES A CENTURY OF FINE SERVICE
TO THE COMMUNITY

Waimatua means *The Source* and from this distinguished source have flowed many famous, interesting and successful people, all of whom have passed through the portals of Waimatua School . . . "

Hey, Mum, what does "portals" mean?'

'Doors. They always say "portals" when it's anything to do with education.'

'Why?'

'They just do.'

'And all that guff about famous and successful people . . . . Is that bullshit, or what?'

'Your father swears it's true, but poetic licence — '

'We got some famous peoples.' Minnie fished in her pile for an envelope. 'Here's Wiremu Hopi. He's with that band *The Whispering Wind*.'

'Never heard of them.'

'They were all the thing a few years back.' She riffled through a few more envelopes. 'Buddy Hohene. He's that golfer. He was on that team that went to South

Africa, eh, and there was all that fuss about them being honorary whites. Remember that?'

'Aaah, not really.'

'Well, we got some guy who's an actor, too. Mary Taki said she seen him on the telly. Some ad about mountain bikes. Nathan somebody. He's about twenty-two, I reckon. Haven't come to him yet. Then there's Darcy Neville.'

Lucille snorted. 'What a name! Sounds like a ponce to me.'

'Shit no. He was one of the greatest fullbacks this country has ever seen. Played 107 test matches for the All Blacks in his time.'

'A hundred and seventeen,' said Pauline, but so quietly neither of them heard her.

'Ace, they called him.'

'*Ace*? Ace Neville? You don't mean that guy with his photograph up in the High School assembly hall?'

'That's him.'

'Shee-ite!'

'*Lucille*!'

'But he's important, Mum! Last year they took the Queen's photo down to put his up in the prime spot. And *he* actually went to our school?'

'You betcha.'

'Wow! He's pretty cool, too. Got a slack hairstyle, parted in the middle and glued down like Winston Peters' but apart from that he's quite a hunk.'

'He *was*,' said Pauline tartly. 'He'll be fat and bald by now, no doubt.'

'Shit, no,' said Minnie. 'There was a picture of him in the *Sunday News*, couple a' weeks back. He don't look no different to when he was eighteen.'

'D'you think he'll come?' wondered Lucille.

'Maybe. If he hears that your mother — '

'That'll do,' quick sharp from Pauline.

Lucille missed it. 'Hey, wouldn't it be awesome if he brought the Whetton twins and John Kirwan with him?'

'They're not in the same generation. He's more your mother's — '

'That's *enough*. Lucille, nip out and put the kettle on, will you? And turn off that racket in your room.'

Lucille sighed. 'Work, work, nothing but work.'

'Tell me about it,' snapped Pauline as Lucille flounced out. She lowered her voice until it shook. 'You can just shut up about Darcy Neville, okay?'

'Keep your hair on. But don't you ever wonder — '

'I mean it, Minnie! *I don't want to know.*'

Billy disbanded tackling practice and came inside in time to watch the direct telecast of a Winfield Cup match from Brisbane. Thomas had dry tears tracked through the dirt on his cheeks.

'Grazed my leg,' he announced, summoning up another sniff. 'Needs a band-aid.'

Pauline sent him off to the shower first. She was proud that he hadn't come running, bawling, when it happened.

The other boys settled on the floor around Billy's chair, ready to watch the league game too, but Pauline shooed them off home.

'Sports players need lots of sleep,' she said.

'Time in bed, anyway,' said Billy. His hand slid up under her skirt.

To cool him she handed him a page of stamps and dumped the bundles in his lap. 'Here. If you stamp the letters they can be posted in the morning.'

'Didn't you do the stamps?'

'Yes we did, but they wanted you to lick them all over again, so they jumped back off the envelopes.'

He squinted at her. 'What's twisting your tits now?'

'Nothing. I'm tired, that's all. Goodnight.' She dropped a kiss onto the top of his head to show she wasn't in a bad mood.

She went into the loo and locked the door. Then she took the envelope addressed to Darcy Neville from under her sweater and ripped it into little pieces into the bowl. It took two goes to flush every bit away.

If she bit her lip hard enough she wouldn't cry. If only she'd been able to get him out of her mind so easily.

Five

'Whaddaya fancy then, Honi?'

Billy was waiting in the public bar for Potu to arrive for their pool game. He wasn't drinking yet. Potu owed him so many rounds that he decided this time for sure he'd tough it out until his brother arrived.

Honi Fells had a *Best Bets*. He was sussing out good prospects for tomorrow's races.

Awhitu Osborne blew a track in his beer froth. He said, 'Stepping Out, I reckon.'

'Stepping Out? Naah,' said Billy. 'That bastard owes me fifty bucks already.'

'Tomorrow he might pay his debts, huh?'

'Be the day.'

'Reckon he's shaping up, eh. Growing into his potential, fullahs said on the radio.'

'Potential? Hah, heard that one before.'

'Could be a champ, they reckon.'

'Yeah, Champ dog food!' Billy laughed at his own joke.

Awhitu laughed too. 'How about sig . . . signif . . . names to do with the Jubilee? Aaah, Centennial, something like that.'

'No Centennial I can see.' Honi was tilting the page towards the light. He could hardly see anything.

'Gizzit.' Billy stood by the window. 'We got a few likely bets here . . . Storm Cloud, Confrontation, Family Quarrel . . . And here's the most likely one; Daggers Drawn.'

Awhitu laughed again. He had a plump smooth face and no teeth. When he laughed he looked like a baby. 'Thought you was in a worse mood than usual. Bad news, committees, eh?'

'Tell me about it.'

'That bad, huh?'

'Not really.' Billy felt edgy. Once the argy-bargy was over and a definite plan of action decided, then it'd be okay.

Michael O'Reay came over with two slopping plastic jugs. 'Your lads have just arrived,' he said to Honi.

Behind him the local motorcycle gang, Death Raiders, were filing in and sprawling at the corner table. There were a dozen or so, lumpy youths with worn-out jeans and black leather jackets with skulls inked in white on the back. Everything about them looked greasy.

Two were Honi's sons, Billy's nephews — wasters, both of them. Billy had coached both boys in the Under Seven Stones when they were nippers but something about them changed when they put on their gang patches. As they pushed the dreadlocks off their faces they gave him thumbs up. Their hands were sprinkled with borstal tats. Rangi's read LOVE HATE across the knuckles while Jamie's message (less successful because of the break in the second word) announced: FUCKY OUALL.

Michael O'Reay watched them out of the corner of his eye. 'Jaysus,' he said. He said it a lot when the gang was there. They made him feel uneasy; the grease on their clothes ground into the seats, they ignored the ashtrays and never used the little white coasters Michael set out for them.

'They're okay,' Awhitu defended them.

'Nothing they do is their fault. Society's against

them,' mocked Billy, who was as edgy around the gang as anyone. Shit but he was in a mood today. It was being close to Bobo every afternoon, breathing in that wonderful wheaty smell of her. Not that he could do or say anything with Lucille right there, sitting across the table, listening. But he could slip her the occasional meaningful look. And he could wait.

'They're good lads,' said Honi.

'Jaysus, my bleeding heart. You'll have me believing in those Maori leprechauns next.'

'Ah, the dainty turehu,' said Billy.

Honi said, 'My boys're okay.' When he was angry his face went hard and flat. 'I dunno what you're on about, mate! *You* can't talk. Where you come from fullahs can't have a jug of piss in peace without some IRA bomb blasting the place.'

'Aye, that's true.' Changing the subject he asked Billy, 'Will you be wantin' a jug of draft?'

Billy dropped his resolution to wait for Potu — the fucker was probably watching through the window until he'd got a jug in — and followed Michael back to the bar.

Larry, the leader of the Death Raiders, loomed up beside him. He was a huge pakeha bloke of around thirty. Australian, Billy had heard. From finger joints to shoulder his left arm was enclosed in a lace mitten of delicately wrought tattoos.

He pulled out a chunk of notes the size of a new bog roll to pay for their drinks. Billy tried not to look at it; he had never seen so much money in one fist before. 'His too,' Larry said, nodding at Billy.

'Well . . . thanks.'

Bits of flax were threaded in the leader's springy hair. He had a row of stars tattooed under one eye. Back in the corner the boys were getting restless, yelling out for their beer.

'You in charge of the Jubilee, mate?'

'Well . . . in a way. I guess so.'

'You'll need lots of help.'

'Tell me about it.'

'Me and the boys could be just what you need.'

Billy was startled. He was too timid to say that what was needed was for the Death Raiders to get on their bikes and go someplace several hundred kilometres away that weekend and stay there until the Jubilee celebrations were over.

The boys started booing. It was all good-natured.

'Me and the boys'd like a job.'

'A job?'

'Yeah, a job. Think on it . . . Spot yer later.' He carried three jugs in each giant fist, back to the table.

'What sort of a job d'you think he meant?'

But Michael O'Reay wasn't listening. He had just figured something out. 'Of course! The dirty bastards. Jaysus! Don't know why I didn't think of it before. It's they'll be the ones who urinate against my wall!'

The gang never stayed long. They breezed in and out like bluebottles. As they left, Potu arrived. The leader turned at the door and gave Billy a thumbs-up, which made him uneasy all over again.

'What's all that about?' said Potu. Plucking himself a glass from the bar he helped himself from Billy's jug.

'They're going to initiate him come Sunday,' said Awhitu. 'He's got to rob a bank and rape an old lady between now and then.'

'Whose old lady, eh?'

'Nah . . . he's the one that'll be raped.'

'Can I watch?' asked Potu.

'Get fucked yourselves,' snapped Billy.

'Got any tips for the races?' Honi wanted to know.

'Parliament,' said Potu in triumph, wiping froth from around his mouth.

'Never heard that word spoken in such a happy tone of voice,' said Billy gloomily.

Outside the bikes roared into a turbulent din.

'Parliament. It's a sure thing for tomorrow, they reckon.'

'Who reckons?' said Billy. 'I seen that thing race twice, and it trailed by a mile both times.'

Awhitu smacked his baby-lips. 'Who gave you the tip?'

Potu was offended. 'Stuff you all. It's just a tip.'

'A rotten one, too.'

Lucille hummed all the time she was washing the dishes. Thomas tried to irk her by slipping plates back into the water and claiming she hadn't washed them properly. She kept right on humming.

'Hi, Foxy Lady,' Felipe Watene had said as she sauntered past to the bus stop.

He was *definitely* talking to her. Not that she took any notice of course. She strolled right on by, pretending she hadn't heard.

She ignored him, just like she was ignoring Thomas now.

'Hi, Foxy Lady,' she hummed under her breath, reliving the moment over and over again.

'You coming along?' Billy wanted to know. He swallowed the dregs of his coffee and left the mug on the bench.

'No thanks.' Pauline had a tracksuit on, and woolly slippers as big as Persian cats. She was knitting something blue. *Coronation Street* was just starting.

'Aaah, come on.'

'No thanks. Minnie always keeps me posted. About everything.'

She was airy-fairy, real sweet, but in her voice something sharp needled like a warning. Lucille wasn't the only spy she had, she seemed to say.

'That's bloody nice of Minnie,' he said.

It was a brilliant idea, Billy reckoned, when he told those at the first meeting to come back with costs for their various schemes. Estimating numbers, getting prices and contacting caterers was work, and who could be bothered? That got rid of the Floating Palace, the Rendezvous Ballroom and a couple of other things right off. And the pub. Billy reported what Michael O'Reay's feelings were, so that idea was scrubbed too.

The Misses Morrison lapsed into prune-faced silence when Billy pointed out that they'd be having their worthwhile suggestions — the picnic, the sports and the hangi —as part of the daytime programme.

For the Big Do then, it came down to a toss-up between the school and the marae.

The marae had a strong backing. It was the heart of Maoridom, which meant the cultural centre of the district, since everyone here, barring the Crawfords and the Morrisons, had some Maori blood. But the meeting house on the marae was a small one, and the adjoining hall was scruffy. The tekoteko lining needed replacing, there were holes punched in the walls, rotting floorboards and leaks in the roof. For years now the

Marae Committee had talked around the question of whether it was worth the expensive repairs it needed, or whether to raise funds for a new one.

Because he'd thought it through, in the end Mr Crawford had his say, and it was decided to use the school. He'd already rung around and discovered that a big marquee could be sent down from a hire firm in Auckland. This would be expensive, but no more so, Mr Crawford pointed out, than the donation they'd have to give the marae if they used it as a venue.

Set up on the edge of the playing field a marquee would be a boon if the weather was wet. Everything from the welcome to the poi dances to the gymnastics display could be held under cover. The marquee would be handy to the classrooms and a clean ablution block — Mr Crawford stressed 'clean' because everybody knew what the toilets at the marae were like.

Mr Crawford had pages of notes. In the classrooms they could set up science displays, an exhibition of artwork and a 'brag board' to pin up articles featured in the *King Country Gazette* over the years about how well the school had done in various inter-school sports carnivals. There were masses of these, all in an album now, but they could be taken out and photocopied.

Mrs Crawford had suggested essay and art competitions for different age groups, including adults, with a theme of the history of school and district. She was willing to go around Te Kuiti and drum up the local businesses to sponsor prizes. The newspaper would print the winning efforts and the prizes could be presented by the Mayor at the dinner-dance.

Mr Crawford had thought of everything, and he

made sure that everyone at the meeting heard about every little detail.

Minnie fidgeted. Minnie liked to be entertained, so she'd never liked Mr Crawford much. Even to look at he was boring, with his beaky face and gangly body. Oh, he was well organised, but you suffered, listening to every little bit of how well he'd organised it all, and how he was paring costs to the bone. Hell, but the man was as tight as a shark's A. H.

Billy doodled all over the borders of his pad and tried not to look at Bobo who was crossing and uncrossing her legs. Her legs were yards of heaven, sheer up to the neatest little arse you could imagine. Billy tried not to imagine it right now.

While Mr Crawford droned on Minnie went outside twice for a ciggie, then didn't come back at all the third time.

It was half-past nine. *Good*, thought Billy, sitting up. With Minnie gone he'd be able to walk Bobo home. He'd make her laugh by telling her he was making sure that she crossed the swing bridge without some sex maniac pouncing on her.

Mr Crawford finished outlining how the morning and afternoon teas could be catered for by teams of parents, each taking turns, and served with a minimum of fuss in one of the classrooms. The food would be served cling-wrapped in saucer-sized portions, each portion containing a small sandwich, a quarter of a standard sandwich slice of corned beef or lettuce and cheese for vegetarians, plus a buttered pikelet and a piece of fruit loaf or a cake of some kind.

Billy thought: Spare us all; he'll be giving us the recipe for pikelets next!

Finally the headmaster finished speaking and

handed his sheaf of notes over to Billy. 'This will save you having to write them up,' he said, smiling with his small, grey teeth.

Billy said, 'Your plan is so comprehensive, Mr Crawford, that I move we adopt it in principle, as is. Allowing for the possibility of minor adjustments, of course, as the need arises.'

'Of course.'

Mrs Crawford beamed as she nodded, her chin bumping against her chest. 'This is so important to Kevin,' she confided to the Morrisons. 'A successful Jubilee will make a good impression for his grading next year.'

There were no matters arising. Nobody felt like talking much after that long monologue.

They broke for supper and Bobo's long legs carried her out to the small kitchenette to make the tea. The Misses Morrison went out to help her set out Krispies and cups. Janey Morrison brought the tea in on a tray. Jessie Morrison passed the plate of biscuits then took a packet of photographs from her bag and bailed the headmaster up with them, cooing, 'I've been meaning to show you these pictures I took in Fiji.'

Tit for tat boredom, thought Billy, drinking his tea.

Mrs Crawford bore down on him. Her son Craig was in the Under Seven Stone rugby team. She didn't like to bring the subject up yet again, she said, not when Billy had so much on his plate with the Jubilee, but he'd have to face facts. The team was going to have to raise money for new jerseys this season. 'It should have been done months ago, as I pointed out at the end of last season.'

And every time you've seen me ever since, thought Billy, mumbling vaguely about getting right onto it. He kept glancing towards the door. Finally he said, 'Where's Bobo?'

'She went home,' Janey Morrison said. 'Poor thing, she's not feeling well.'

Billy felt like kicking something. 'Tell me about it,' he said.

Six

Everybody waiting outside Firplace Furnishings was grumbling because they had to stocktake on raceday. Pauline couldn't care less; to her, horse racing was just another way of throwing money away.

To keep warm she walked up and down the storefront. In the corner window was the bedroom suite she desired. It had a highboy and a long, low dressing-table with a huge oval mirror. The finish was walnut, with a gloss as thick as golden syrup. She tried to picture it in the bedroom at home, and laughed.

'What's the joke?' asked Arthur Nimwood from accounts. He was about her age, but to her seemed like a schoolboy.

'I was thinking how out-of-place this would look in my room.'

'Why?'

That was his way: he questioned everything. A right smartarse. Got up everybody's nose.

'Because the room needs redecorating, of course.' That was an understatement. She could have told him about the stained ceiling, the tatty curtains and that mess along one wall where Thomas as a toddler had scribbled all over the paper with a ball-point pen. Her efforts to get it off only made it worse.

'We sell wallpaper and paint, too, you know.'

'My husband is far too busy right now.'

'Why does it need to be him?'

'Who else would do it?'

He just looked at her. He had pale eyes and pale skin.

'What? You mean *me* paint and paper?'

'Why not?'

'Because it's not my job, that's why.'

He smiled. 'If you want something done in life, often times you have to do it yourself.'

She had to laugh at that. 'I couldn't.'

'Ah, but you don't know what you're capable of unless you try. A positive attitude is all you need.'

Her eyes rolled up; she was sorry she talked to him in the first place. Arthur was a New Age thinker, into self-realisation, meditation and all that nonsense. A Giant Pain. He was always spouting gems like: 'If you always do what you've always done, you'll always get what you've always got.' Which Pauline thought was stupid. You did what you did because that was the best way you knew.

She did the housekeeping, Billy did the outside and the maintenance.

The problem was how to get him to do anything at all these days. A positive attitude? Ha! What she needed was a stick of dynamite to shove up his lazy arse.

When they saw Lucille waiting by the pickup and ready to go to the races, Minnie and Potu came over. Potu was wearing a jacket and a hat.

'Hey, you look cool,' said Lucille. 'One cool dude.'

Minnie squeaked with mirth. 'It's a pork-pie hat. If he gets hungry, he can eat it, eh?'

'Shuddup, eh.'

Lucille looked from one to the other. Minnie's shadow flopped clear over Potu like a tent. The impossibility of sex between them still bothered her. Without thinking she blurted, 'How come you two got no kids?'

45

'Tried it once and didn't like it,' said Potu.

'I should be so lucky!'

'You mean sex?' asked Lucille. 'You only tried sex once?'

Potu sidled over. His round eyes were shifty with embarrassment.

'Hey, girlie, you's too young to ask them kinda questions.'

Billy was still inside, helping Thomas look for his shoes. Minnie lit up a ciggie. 'What bullshit's that bloody liar telling you?'

Potu twirled his hat and snapped the brim. 'What I said, Jack Nohi, is that if we had any kids they'd pop out in Winfields packets.'

'Aaah, stop playing that old record or I'll smash it.'

'Uncle Potu's right, you know. Smoking is terribly bad for you.'

'So is screwing. I never heard him nagging me about that. Not one bloody time!'

'You could get lung cancer and die, Auntie. Honest.'

'I could get cancer of the U-know-what, too. They's said so on telly, eh. On the news. . . Too much sex can give you's certifiable cancer.'

'Cervical.' From Lucille.

'Whatever.'

'Auntie Minnie, it didn't mean too *much* sex. It means too many different men. If a woman indulges with more than two or three partners, besides the risk of sexually transmitted diseases, she runs a higher-than-average chance — '

Astounded, Minnie cut in. 'You sound like a bloody medical book! How the hell do you know all this stuff?'

'Miss Pring taught us in Hygiene class. She said that even with the precaution of using condoms — '

Potu's eyes were huge with shock. 'Waitaminute! Lemme get this straight, eh. They *teach* you's all this dirty stuff at school?'

'It's not dirty, eh. Sex is perfectly natural.'

'You's listen here, girlie. There's nothing perfect about sex, and for that matter there's nothing dirtier than nature, and that's the truth. Okay?'

Minnie squeaked, 'Yeah, listen to him, kid. He's an expert on the subject, eh.'

He reached over to slap her. She ducked away, giggling so much that her stomach shuddered like a pup tent in a high wind.

Raceday was a family affair. For the kiddies they had hotdog stands, doughnuts, chips and drinks stalls. A ferris wheel and a merry-go-round churned around behind the grandstand. Their music see-sawed between the blatted-out announcements of each race.

For the grown-ups there was beer. Huge plastic jugs of the stuff. 'Your shout,' said Billy as they pushed through the throng around the bar in the refreshment hall.

'Right,' said Potu. 'In a minute. You's find somewhere to sit. First I gotta see a man about a dog.'

Minnie went off to shake a packet of Winfield Blue out of the vending machine.

Bloody great, thought Billy. He bought the drinks.

Lucille and Thomas wandered about outside. Each had five dollars to spend. Thomas blew his in five minutes at the shooting gallery, then he and the Taki kids collected discarded tote tickets and scanned them to see if anybody had dropped a live one by mistake.

Nobody had.

Lucille bought a puff of candyfloss. She saw Elsie and Betty Watene with some of their classmates, and hurried over to them. If Dennis and Felipe saw her talking to their sisters they might stop and talk too. The girls were sighing over the hunks on *Baywatch* from on telly the night before. They grabbed the candyfloss and bit into it.

Lucille wiped the sticky shreds off her cheeks. 'I never get to see that. Mum has to have her fix of *Coronation Street* and it's on at the same time. Slack, eh?'

As she talked she kept glancing around, scanning the crowd.

Betty said, 'Ain't you fullahs got a video?'

'Naah. We had one but it was hired. Dad caught Thomas watching porn, so he sent it back to the shop. Dunno why he bothered — Thomas sees heaps down at the Takis' place. Reckons they're slack.'

'Some of them aren't bad,' said Betty.

'Do they have any with fat people — '

Elsie grabbed her sister's arm. 'Quick. Let's split. There's our stupid brothers.'

They ran giggling towards the ferris wheel. Disappointed, Lucille tagged after them.

Bobo was by the merry-go-round, watching the twins ride. She was wearing a bright pink leather jacket and a micro-miniskirt with spindly pink shoes. Lucille liked Mrs Penny, but she looked wistfully at her clothes and thought: *What a waste. All those awesome threads on an old woman like her.*

'Hello, Lucille love. Yer mum here?'

'Nah, she's working.'

'Oh...' Her eyes slid past Lucille. 'Where's yer dad?'

'In the refreshment hall.'

'Right.' She winked at Lucille. 'I'll be careful then.'

'Wow, those clothes are really excellent, eh. Who's she?' said Elsie as they moved away.

'My dad's ex-mistress,' said Lucille loftily. She wasn't sure if it was true, but that didn't matter. It didn't half make them blink.

It was one of Billy's worst days ever, if not *the* worst. From the hundred bucks he'd brought to invest there was only a ten-dollar note and a shoal of change left. Potu had made four hundred bucks. He was crowing like that bloody rooster over his winnings, rubbing it in except when there were drinks to buy. Billy was so mad about that, he could hit something. If it was one of his mates he'd be pleased and pat him on the back, make him cough up for a few rounds, but Potu's success was hard to take.

Billy walked away and considered his bets for the last race. He scanned the telly, reading names and form. Parliament. That loser, he thought, remembering the hoots of derision at the pub.

He read the other names. Nothing inspiring. Almost all of them owed him money. He looked at Parliament again. Its form was lousy. Nowhere from the last five starts. The odds were a joke, nine hundred to one.

He looked again, trying to find something that fitted with the Jubilee and the committee. Then he thought: Parliament. That's a kind of a committee, right?

Despair made him reckless. He was down the tubes for almost ninety bucks, so what the hell, he thought as he counted out his change, marched out to the tote window, and put fourteen dollars on Parliament. To win.

As he took his ticket he felt clean and light. He didn't even notice the gang standing a few yards back from the window until he'd walked right in amongst them.

The leader clapped him on the back. 'Thought about a job for us, yet?'

Billy nearly wet himself. 'Aaah, I'll put it to the parliament—I mean, the *committee* at the next meeting.'

Billy didn't believe it. He felt as if he was in a sealed jar, and everything happening outside was blurry. All around him people were flinging down their tote tickets in disgust. Potu was furious. 'It fucking *romped home*! I should'a listened!' he moaned. 'Bloody fucking hell, I should'a listened.'

Six thousand four hundred dollars! Billy *couldn't* believe it. His fourteen dollars on Parliament had won him six thousand four hundred dollars.

He didn't speak. It seemed too unreal. He'd get the money in his hand first and believe it after he'd counted it.

Six thousand, four hundred dollars!

'Gotta strain the potatoes,' he told Minnie and Potu.

'Don't strain yourself,' said Minnie.

'I'll come too,' said Potu.

He couldn't piss. He didn't half feel stupid standing by Potu and nothing happening. Potu noticed but he didn't say anything.

'Gotta find the kids,' he said as they left the refreshment hall. He had to get away, collect the money without anybody knowing.

'Here they are,' said Minnie.

In the stream of homebound punters they drifted past the pay-out window. Billy tried to think of an excuse to turn back, but then he saw the gang still hanging around there, watching everybody who went to collect their winnings.

Six thousand four hundred dollars!

He kept on walking.

'Hey, Foxy Lady!'

Lucille glanced around. Felipe Watene was smiling at her. He put his tongue between his teeth. She didn't know what that meant, but it looked wicked.

She could feel her face going scarlet.

She hurried past, very quickly.

Back at the pub, Potu paid for the drinks for once. He thought Billy was depressed on account of blowing all his dough. He'd never known him so quiet.

Not that he was celebrating. He might have won more than ever before, but all he could think of was how stupid he'd been. To think he had been given the tip, and he hadn't had the nous to act on it. He felt like bloody bawling.

'Six thousand bucks, eh,' he said to Billy.

'Eh?'

'Wake up, eh . . . Whaddaya reckon you could do with six thousand bucks?'

'Dunno,' said Billy. He still couldn't believe it. This was crazy. He should feel fucking marvellous, but he felt scared and shaky instead.

As they wove out to the ute he realised he was drunk as a skunk. He leaned on the wall. It smelled of pine disinfectant. He unzipped his fly.

Aaaaah! This was better. He felt human again. He felt great. There was a moon shining over his shoulder; the warm smell of urine wafting up around him. There was nothing like this feeling of letting it all go out in the fresh air with the stars whirling above, being one with the universe.

'Bloody wunnerful,' he said to Potu. 'Wonder why they alwaysh write songs about how good sex feels but never about pissing?'

He began to sing, off key, 'I'm PISSED! I been drinking PISS . . . so don't take the PISS or you can PISS OFF!'

'Michael O'Reay won't half be pissed if he catches you, either,' said Potu.

'He doesn't piss, he U-ROI-NOITES,' said Billy. This seemed wildly funny to him.

Potu caught Billy as he stumbled, piled him into the back seat of the ute so's he wouldn't try to grab the wheel, and drove them both home.

Seven

It figured, thought Billy. Now that they were getting to the nitty-gritty only five others showed up for the next committee meeting; Mr and Mrs Crawford, Bobo, Minnie, Potu and himself.

Bobo reported that Jessie Morrison had phoned to say that Janey had a cold, so's she thought it best if they both stayed home. So's not to spread germs.

'So's not to spread work, you mean,' said Minnie. 'If they showed up they might catch some.'

There were no apologies from Awhitu or any of the others. The All Blacks were touring France and the Winfield Cup games had started across the Tasman. Unless Michael O'Reay splashed out on one of those giant-screened TVs the crowd would be thin, even at the pub on broadcast nights.

'Maybe we should change the meeting night,' said Bobo.

'Let's see how we get on, first, ' suggested Mr Crawford. 'Once we've settled the budget tonight, we can think about the nuts and bolts of what needs doing. Then all we need to do is go out into the community and delegate.'

Billy had to be reminded to call the meeting to order. He'd been in a daze all week. *Six thousand four hundred dollars!* The whole district was buzzing over someone's lucky win, and speculation was rife as to who that person might be.

The money was still uncollected and the tote ticket

still in a little plastic bag sticking-plastered to the skin on his side, up under his arm. He kept checking that it hadn't come loose. What a bitch if that happened!

Twice he'd driven past the Te Kuiti branch of the TAB on his way home from work, but both times the big black Harley Davidsons belonging to the Death Raiders were parked outside, so he gunned the ute straight past. He wondered if their presence was a coincidence, or if they were waiting to see who the lucky punter was.

He tried to concentrate on the meeting. Bobo reported that in response to the first mailing, they had received twenty-two requests for more information. Billy thought that was poor but Mr Crawford said the interest shown was 'extraordinary'.

'Ace Neville hasn't sent his back,' said Minnie, thumbing through the letters. 'Maybe he's not coming. Maybe he thinks he's too good for us, eh?'

'It's early days yet,' said Mr Crawford. 'But it's time to get on with the next step.'

From then on the headmaster virtually took over. He might be the most boring old fart on the face of the earth but he knew his figures, allowed Billy. In half an hour they had a budget with built-in allowances for all the contingencies they could think of.

A band for the 'do' — five hundred dollars was what The Dreamers were asking. Potu was outraged. He said he'd get them for a bottle of whisky apiece by reminding them of their loyalty to the district.

Mr Crawford thought that was a good idea.

Billy said they'd hire them properly. 'We want a civilised function, not a brawl with a drunken band. If you pay peanuts, you'll get monkeys. And if you pay booze, you'll get piss-heads.'

You couldn't get a button through Mrs Crawford's lips. Then she enunciated, 'Thank you, Mr Williams. A valid point, if a little crudely expressed.'

Minnie squeaked. Good on Billy! The Crawfords were too up-themselves sometimes. Mr Crawford said, 'Tell the meeting what you've been doing, dear.'

Looking pleased with herself, Mrs Crawford reported that she'd approached General Foods and had been promised generous support for grocery items: frozen peas and vegetables for the dinner, flour and other goods for the home baking for morning teas and bread for the sandwiches.

'I've written away to the Chelsea Sugarworks and to the tea and coffee importers,' she added. 'And I thought we could ask local farmers for some produce.'

Billy made a list on the blackboard — pork (they might have to offer a few bucks in exchange on account of pork being so expensive), lamb (no problem with that), potatoes, cabbage and pumpkin for the hangi, and chooks and eggs.

Bobo copied it all down.

Mrs Crawford suggested that they could approach all the farmers in the district for pledges, and once they had a rough idea of numbers attending, they could work out exactly what was needed. Everybody agreed that was a good idea.

Mr Crawford said that with the projected stationery and copying expenses, postage, ads in newspapers around the country, marquee hire, cutlery and crockery hire, glassware and the band they had a preliminary total of two thousand eight hundred and fifty dollars.

'Shivering shit,' said Billy, intercepting a cool glare from Mrs Crawford. 'If only fifty people come, that's sixty bucks each!'

'Fifty-seven,' corrected Mr Crawford. 'But I think we can guarantee at least a hundred registrations.'

'So we charge them each twenty-eight dollars?'

'We could. But there could easily be cost over-runs and unforeseen expenses. I thought that forty dollars a head would be a reasonable fee.'

Bobo and Minnie both thought it was too high. If they charged too much, then nobody would come.

Billy pointed out that for that one payment they'd be getting two lunches, morning and afternoon teas, a hangi, a feed, an evening's entertainment —

'If you call boring speeches entertainment!' interjected Minnie.

Billy went on with his list: a commemorative booklet and full participation in the weekend's activities. A bargain by anybody's standards.

But Minnie had a point there, suggested Potu. Perhaps they should jack up an act or two as well as the band. Not everybody liked dancing but everyone appreciated a good laugh.

'That could add considerably to the cost.'

'Nah,' Potu told the headmaster. 'There's lots of talent in the district. We'll jack something up, eh.'

'We'll leave that in your capable hands, then . . . But the committee must have the right of veto. There must be nothing smutty, you understand.'

'We must keep the tone up,' agreed his wife.

Potu thought, *Bloody hell . . . I should've stayed home to watch the Winfield Cup.*

They drafted the registration forms and moved that Bobo and Billy get them into the post.

The meeting closed. Bobo went into the kitchenette to make the tea. Billy was about to follow her when Mrs Crawford bailed him up about the football jerseys.

'Have you given any thought to fund-raising?'

He hadn't. He nodded. 'A raffle, I thought.'

She looked disappointed at his lack of imagination. 'Maybe a working bee of some kind?'

Minnie said, 'Has anyone heard who won that big payout yet?'

'Someone out-of-town they reckon,' said Bobo, pouring.

'An amazing stroke of luck,' said Mr Crawford.

'Amazing,' said Billy.

'Potu's been spitting blood, haven't you eh? He had the tip but the stupid bugger never listened, eh.'

'Mrs Renshaw can't recall who bought the ticket, but she's sure it's a man,' reported Mrs Crawford. She took two Krispies and put them neatly on her saucer.

'Weird that he hasn't collected it, eh?'

'Maybe he's lost the ticket,' mused Bobo.

Billy quickly patted under his arm. Through his shirt the plastic crinkled. Just in time he stopped himself from blurting: *Don't scare me like that*!

'What would you do if you won that amount of money, Billy?' asked Bobo.

'I don't honestly know,' said Billy seriously.

Bobo stared at him. 'You look awful. As if you hadn't slept for a month.'

Billy leered at her. If she knew what was really keeping him awake nights she'd be over him like a rash. 'My life's too excitin' for sleep, darlin',' he said.

'How do really fat people do it?' Lucille asked Thomas. She was whispering. Their mother was in the kitchen, cutting tomorrow's lunches. 'I mean really, awesomely fat.'

Thomas wasn't listening. *Coca-Cola Top Twenty Hits*

was on the telly and he was letting it all loosen down with Hammer.

She elbowed him. He elbowed her. 'How do fat people get it off?' she asked again.

'Get what off?'

'You know! Fucking.'

He glanced at her but immediately lost the brief flicker of interest. 'Dunno. Same as anybody else.' He shrugged his shoulders, flapped his arms, grooving with the music. Hammer was jumping from one rock to another. His knees were apart. He looked like an elegant scarlet frog.

'*Awesome*!'

Lucille gave up.

As he pulled into the driveway, Billy had a brainwave. He'd make an extra early start so's he could knock off early and drive up to Hamilton to collect his winnings. In a city TAB nobody would notice him. Hamilton was surrounded by race-horse country. Big winnings were commonplace. Word would filter back that the six thousand four hundred dollars had been claimed. Soon it would be common knowledge that someone outside of the King Country had scooped that massive win. For years to come people would think back, trying to remember strangers who had been at the race meeting.

Nobody would ever guess it was him.

Days were colder now. When Lucille sat on the steps while Minnie brushed her hair she noticed that the hillsides were turning the colour of toast. Her three chooks strutted about with their feathers fluffed out. Doc's comb was definitely growing.

Lucille showed Minnie a picture in a *Jackie* magazine.

The girl in the picture had a long ponytail, like Lucille's, with fine braids worked through it. Beads and ribbons studded the braids.

'Can you style it like that for the big do?'

'Piece of cake, by the looks. You's sure you don't want a French plait?'

'Naa . . . no thanks. They're nerdy now.'

'Nerdy, trendy . . . ' Minnie giggled. Her stomach nudged Lucille's back.

'Auntie Minnie?'

'Wha?'

'I really like you . . . nah, I really love you, y'know?'

'Get away.' But she sounded pleased. And she hugged Lucille.

When Minnie hugged it felt great. Like being wrapped in a big, soft duvet. Maybe Uncle Potu sort of sank into her, she mused.

Pauline offered to take the registration forms to be posted. She was going to leaf through them on the bus and take Darcy Neville's out, but Mary Taki was on the bus too, yakkety-yakking all the way into town, so she couldn't do anything, not with that sticky-beak watching.

The bus was late, too. Outside the store she frantically shuffled the envelopes, fumbled, and spilled them all over the pavement.

'Here, let me help.' Shit! It was Arthur Nimwood.

'No, really, no! No thanks!'

But before she could stop him he'd scooped them up in his bustling busy-body way.

'Thanks.' She reached out to take them.

'No trouble, dear lady.' *And he posted them all*! She had to stand by the window, staring at the glossy bedroom suite and blinking back cold and angry tears until she recovered enough to go and clock in.

Seeing her reflection in the dressing table mirror didn't help much either. Her warm red trouser suit had a wonky, homemade look around the collar. *Face it lady, you can't sew.*

Her hair was a tangle of sticking-out wisps.

Face it lady, you're no beauty.

She thought about her life. Her bedroom with the stains on the ceiling and the tatty curtains and the mess where she'd tried to get the biro scrawl off the wallpaper. She thought about that dismal back yard, about the car that wasn't ever going to get fixed. The husband who would need a bomb to get motivated.

Face it lady, your life's a disaster area.

During her lunch break Arthur came and sat beside her.

'Make yourself at home,' she said.

'Thanks.' Sarcasm was lost on him. 'I saw you staring at the walnut ensemble this morning. Have you had a change of heart?'

'I told you, it would look out of place unless the room was redecorated.' She stared at her coffee mug but she could feel him watching her. It was like having a wasp crawling over her skin. She said, 'My husband hasn't time. He works very hard, I'll have you know.'

'Harder than you?'

He had a point there. A sharp point. It made her blink, as if he'd jabbed her with it.

It made her think, too. Billy was the one with time to spare to go to the races, to booze at the pub, to be chairman of committees. Aaaah, she thought as she rinsed the mug and dried it. What was the use in stirring things? No use all.

'Why not have a go yourself?' said Arthur Nimwood softly.

Why not fuck yourself? she thought as she left the room.

But now that her resentment was exposed, she picked at it like a scab.

Billy was late home from the pub again. She wanted to go to bed but stayed up so's he wouldn't have to eat dinner on his own. It was roast lamb with baked potato, mashed pumpkin and peas with lashings of gravy. It was a lot more trouble to make gravy, but Billy liked it. She'd made mint jelly, too, with added walnuts and pineapple from a recipe in one of Minnie's magazines.

'D'you like it? Bit different, huh? I rubbed mustard and brown sugar on the meat before it went into the oven.'

'Yeah, yeah, it's great!'

'What's wrong, Billy?'

'Whaddaya mean?'

'You seem different. Nothing wrong, is there?'

He knew she was asking if there was somebody else. Pauline'd never come right out and ask him straight. There was always this sideways approach.

As soon as they got into bed he proved quick smart that her suspicions were wrong. Afterwards, when she thought he'd gone to sleep, Pauline cried and cried. Even their sex was rotten these days — just a stab in the dark, careless and unfinished like everything else Billy did.

I had dreams once, she kept thinking. *I had dreams, and now look at what's happened to my life.*

Eight

On Pauline's fortieth birthday the rural delivery van dropped off a five-litre ice cream container of whitebait, sent from up the coast by Billy's older sister Nefta and from Granny, their mother. They knew that Pauline didn't like whitebait, but sent the same gift every year.

From Thomas she received a big box of Thomas's favourite chocolate fish, while Minnie and Potu gave her a sweater with cats appliquéd on the front.

She loved the housecoat. Lucille stood beside her, twisting the ends of her hair while she opened the parcel. It was the only one wrapped up with a ribbon.

Billy gave her a bright pink leather jacket. 'They seem to be what's trendy now,' he said.

'Awesome!' breathed Lucille, planning to borrow it.

Being Billy he had left the docket in the box. *Hamilton*! she thought, dismayed that it was such a long way to go to return it. Then she saw the price — eight hundred dollars — and the ABSOLUTELY NO REFUNDS stamp across the docket, and burst into tears. She couldn't stop herself; what she could do with eight hundred dollars didn't bear thinking about.

Quite forgetting it was identical to Bobo's, Billy thought she was pleased. He'd bought the jacket right after cashing the ticket. The leather fashions shop was right next door to the TAB and he'd dived in there to check if he was being followed. By the time the jacket was wrapped up he was regretting his impulsive purchase. He'd never splurged like that before; she'd think he had a guilty conscience.

This money business was weird. It was exhilarating to splash money out, but a few seconds later worry set in. The roll of cash became a liability beyond anything he could have imagined.

All the way home he fretted about having an accident. Suppose he was lying unconscious in the wreckage and someone pinched his wallet? That very thing happened on a *Crimewatch* reconstruction last month when some bastard rolled a victim of a hit-and-run. Pulling over, Billy took the money from his wallet and wedged it out of sight up under the seat.

When he got home his insecurity ballooned. He shifted the money from one hiding place to another. Suppose they were robbed? Suppose there was a fire? Cash wasn't covered by insurance. He hid it in the ute then worried that the ute might be stolen. He fretted all the time. Banking it was out of the question. The news would be all around the district by dinnertime.

At night it was worse, because in the dark anything seemed possible. Maybe the Death Raiders already knew about his win? Maybe someone in the Hamilton TAB recognised him? There could have been a gang spy there. There could have been a tip-off. Even now he could be under surveillance. Maybe the Death Raiders knew his every move? Maybe they planned to get him alone and beat him until he handed the money over?

If it wasn't so frightening, the irony would be funny. All his life he'd imagined how great it would be to strike a big win, but the reality was a nightmare. The only good part so far was listening to Potu moaning about how he'd missed out on that sure thing.

'You won four hundred, so what's the problem?'

said Billy. 'I blew my dough, but d'you hear me complain? Here, you get the next round, you owe me about a tanker load. Time you started paying me back.'

He'd never have talked to his older brother like that before. Having money, even secret money, gave him a sense of power.

'What have you got there?'

Arthur Nimwood really was a pain in the arse. Without a by-your-leave he pulled the pink leather jacket out of the box and looked at the docket.

'I'm selling it. I'd never wear it.'

'But it's beautiful. Don't you think you deserve it?'

I don't want to strut around looking like Bobo Penny's older, uglier sister! 'Pink's not my colour.'

Before she could stop him Arthur was on the phone. Over his shoulder he said, 'Does it fit? Do you like the style?' and five minutes later he'd arranged for the shop to exchange it for a red one. They could do the swap by bus.

'You cheeky bastard!' Pauline was astounded. 'The way you just do anything you want.'

'You can too, you know. Don't tell me you aren't pleased.'

She tried hard to feel annoyed but this time she couldn't.

'Too much on my plate, that's what's the matter,' said Billy. He and Awhitu, Potu and Honi were sinking jugs in the public bar.

'Trouble with life, no fucking time to do anything,' agreed Awhitu.

'Even fuck,' said Honi.

'Always find time for that,' said Potu.

'Biggest time-waster of the lot,' said Awhitu. 'It's all the stuff you's gotta do to get them in the mood.'

Billy was feeling too gloomy to boast that he could get Pauline in the mood just by giving her the right look. Never had the smallest problem there.

His worries were different. He'd sent a letter home with all the schoolchildren asking for volunteers from the parents for the long list of Jubilee tasks, but so far the only response was a query from Mrs Crawford asking what progress had been made on the team jerseys. What with the win and everything, it had gone out of his head. What a bugger. Practice started Thursday afternoon, with the first game of the season against Taumarunui two Saturdays away.

He was deep in gloomy contemplation when a hand clapped on to his shoulder. Honi's face opposite should have alerted him that something was wrong. He glanced around and saw the delicate mitten tattoos. Larry of the Death Raiders loomed over him.

Billy nearly wet himself. He choked on a mouthful of beer. *He's on to me!* he thought.

'Lined up a job for the boys yet, mate?'

Mate! Billy shuddered in relief. 'Aaah, not yet.'

'Not yet?'

'Early days yet.'

'Me an' the boys been talking. What you need is some good security.'

'You're joking. This is a tinpot school jubilee, not a rock concert, man.' Billy glanced at the others but they were all suddenly concentrating on their beer.

'You need security, mate, believe me. So's people won't get mugged. So's their cars won't get ripped off. So's there's no gatecrashers. Think about it. Spot you later.'

'Shit,' said Potu in a whisper.

'You said it,' said Billy. Whenever there was an outbreak of petty crime in the district, the gang was always blamed, and rightly too. Who else would rip off cars, commit robberies?

'What he said to you . . . That's protection, ain'it? Mafia stuff.'

'What can I do?'

'Make like an Eyetie, eh,' advised Potu.

'What's that?'

'You's do what they say, of course.'

The others laughed. Billy didn't laugh.

'Jaysus, those bastards are at it again,' complained Michael O'Reay as he refilled their jugs with the draught nozzle. 'This time I saw them with my own eyes. All in a row, they was, like blackbirds on a clothesline, urinating against me wall.'

'Filthy bastards,' agreed Billy.

'Trouble is,' mused Billy, as he and Potu stood there later, performing the same act in the moonlight. 'Michael O'Reay is a good bloke, eh, but he keeps that bog of his too clean. I mean a bog should be down-to-earth, right? Comfortable, like. Not shiny and perfumed.'

'I know what you mean,' said Potu.

As he shook himself, Billy waxed philosophical. 'It's the aesthetics of it, eh.'

'Anaesthetics?'

'Nah, you moron, *aesthetics*. The sense of beauty. In there, it feels all wrong — like taking a leak in church.'

Pauline took a taxi home. It cost her sixteen dollars but it was the only way she could manage the drums of white paint and the cartons of wallpaper rolls.

Billy arrived home to find all the furniture piled in

the porch. He had to bang on the ranchslider until Thomas let him in. Lucille was lying on the double mattress on the living room floor watching TV. 'This is neat fun. Like camping,' she said.

The kitchen smelled weird. There was nothing in the oven, no prepared food in the fridge. Music blasted from the bedroom.

'Where's me fucking dinner?'

'We had bread and jam and ice cream,' Thomas reported.

'Thomas finished up the ice cream, but there's plenty of bread,' Pauline told him, shouting above the noise of *Crowded House*. The weird smell was paint. Pauline was up a stepladder, slopping rollersful of the stuff across the bedroom ceiling. She wore one of his old shirts over her clothes, and had her hair up under a showercap. Old sheets were spread wall-to-wall. Everything was speckled with dandruffy spots.

'What the hell's this, then?'

'What the hell's what?'

'Since when has decorating been your job?'

'Okay. If it's yours, you do it.'

They stared at each other until Billy looked away. His empty stomach churned with frustration and anger. What a typical bloody pakeha female trick: to start something when he had no hope of retaliating.

'You know I'm too damned busy to paint and wallpaper now!'

'Okay,' she said cheerfully. 'I'm surprised, actually. This is fun.'

His stomach churned again. 'So much fun that you've forgotten to cook dinner?'

'I didn't forget. I was just too busy. There's plenty of bread and jam. That's what we had.' She rocked her bum to the music and sang, Take the weather . . . '

'Shit Pauline! I'm a working man!'

'I do a full-time job too.'

'But I hate bread and jam.'

'Then cook something!'

He shut the door, dazed, then realised that in all their marriage she had never acted like this before. As if she didn't care. As if his needs didn't count for anything. He couldn't have been more outraged if she'd dumped the paint over his head. She wasn't supposed to *be* like this, dammit!

Opening the door he shouted, 'And fuck you, too!' then slammed it shut again. It wasn't original. It wasn't clever. The worst part was, it didn't even make him feel better.

'I got sponsorship for the jerseys,' Billy told Mrs Crawford at the next meeting of the Jubilee Committee. He was so pissed off with everything that when her fourth message in four days came he thought to hell with it, and took another four hundred dollars from the hoard.

She said nothing for ages, just looked at the cash. Made a change from staring at his unironed shirt and rumpled trousers, he thought.

'I know it's not the full amount, but I figured they could earn the rest . . . you know, individually, eh.' That was the way they usually operated.

She sounded sniffy. Annoyed, even. He wondered why, until she burst out, 'Billy, this is unbelievable. I've been trekking back and forth through town for weeks, scrounging up sponsors for the Jubilee, and never raised a fraction of this amount. How in the world did you do it?'

She's jealous! She thinks I've stolen her thunder. 'Ah
. . . It's because it's for a sports team, I suppose.'

Her lips buttoned up tight. 'You've hit the nail on the
head. That's what's wrong with this country. Sports are
everything. Nobody's interested in the higher pursuits
in life. But tell me, who is the source of this generosity?
We'd better have his name on the jerseys.'

'Ah . . . Ah . . . he wants to be anonymous.'

'That's ridiculous! The whole purpose of being a
sponsor — '

'That's what I said, too. Excuse me, Mrs Crawford,
but we'd better call the meeting to order.'

'Security?' repeated Mr Crawford.

He had the knack of making Billy feel that he was
still a little boy at school, fidgeting at the blackboard
with old Mr Hurton standing over him with his long,
switchy bamboo cane. It wasn't the cane that paralysed
Billy's mind, but the look in Mr Hurton's eyes. Kevin
Crawford had that same look in those yellowy eyes of
his. As if he was being lied to. Incredulous, yet piercing.

Billy stammered out the details of his conversations
with the Death Raiders while Mr Crawford's face looked
more beaky and piercing.

'What you're saying is that the gang are leaning on
you. All this talk of preventing muggings, car conversion
and so on is nothing more than a veiled threat.'

'I'm just passing on the message.'

'I don't know why you bothered. That's mob tactics.
A matter for the police.' His eyes gleamed with malice.
'I move that Mr Williams should place a formal
complaint with the Te Kuiti police.' He glanced at his
wife.

'I second that,' she said quickly.

'Whaddaya going to do about the gang?' asked Potu later at the pub.

'Nothing,' said Billy, topping up his glass. 'I plan to go on breathing. I'm certainly not going to the police. Stuff that!'

'You'll have to do something about the job then, eh. They'll fix you's but good if you ignore them.'

'Thanks for the glad tidings,' said Billy gloomily. His life was turning to shit and he didn't have a shovel.

'Your round,' he said, drawing a small crumb of satisfaction where he could. 'We're nowhere near even yet.'

Nine

'Paulie . . . ' Billy approached her sweetly. She was on a stepladder in the kitchen now. 'I wondered if you'd mind helping me with — '

'Sorry. I'm too busy.'

'Come on, Paulie.' He opened the folder containing rough sketches of a poster that needed final artwork. 'It'll only take a few minutes. You know what my art's like, and it would be so easy for you. Surely you could help.'

'Sorry.'

Damn it. She wouldn't even look at it. He'd hoped to leave it with her and slope over to Potu's to watch the Test.

As if she guessed his motives she said, 'Maybe you could have Potu help you while you're watching the game?'

That really burned him. He tried to think of some way to lash back at her for reading him so easily. 'Are you sure you posted all those registration forms?'

'Wha . . . ?' Pauline nearly fell off the stepladder.

He grabbed her legs to balance her. Billy was getting used to this view of her. Let's face it, he thought, a view of her legs was all he was bloody getting these days. No lunches cut, no meals cooked, no laundry done. The bedroom was painted and papered but without furniture, so they were still sleeping in right royal discomfort on the floor. Sex? Ha bloody ha! He'd forgotten what a nookie felt like.

'The registration forms. Those envelopes. Did you post them?'

'Course I did. Why?'

It occurred to him that she looked guilty, and he wondered why.

'Because we haven't had any registrations, that's why.'

'None at all?'

'Only one or two. But — '

'There you are then.' In trying to wipe a smear of paint off her cheek with the shirt-tail she only made it worse. 'You haven't had more than that because most people are like you.'

'What's that supposed to mean?'

'The Jubilee's still well over a month away. You never register for anything till the last minute either, so why should they?'

That was below the belt. 'Renewing my subs to the RSA is different.'

'Is it?'

'Course it is.'

'If you say so, then. Ah . . . I sure could murder a cup of tea.'

Billy grinned. He'd been waiting for this, a chance to say, 'Then brew it yourself.' Hand her back some of the crap she'd been dishing him the last few weeks.

He couldn't bloody win. Before he could speak Lucille said from behind him, 'Okay, Mum.'

'Kettle's in the wash house. You'll need to boil it out there. Use that black extension cord and plug it into the hall socket.'

'Okay. D'you want a cuppa too, Dad?' She was singing as she left the room.

'She's in a good mood.' Just as well someone was.

'She's in love. I found a photo under the pillow when I stripped her bed this morning.'

Relieved to be able to focus his irritation on something, Billy blurted, 'But she's only fourteen! What's his name? I'll soon fix — '

Pauline wagged the paintbrush at him. 'You leave her alone, d'you hear? She's got to grow up, and we agreed to let her do it in her own way, at her own pace, remember? Lucille's a sensible girl. Besides, he looks like a nice boy.'

Billy started to argue, then gave up. He hated to think of Lucille growing up, but even worse he hated what was happening to Pauline. She was suddenly so positive about everything, and that made him feel insecure. On the one hand it was nice to have all this decorating done — she was making a good job, too – but the way she neglected him without seeming to care really rocked his sense of husbandly self-worth.

How could a woman suddenly change like this?

Muttering to himself he hurried along the path through the weeds to Potu's house. It wasn't right, but these days he felt more comfortable there than in his own home.

On and off for more than a month now he'd been mulling over the information Rangi Kaawa gave him, planning how best to stir some genuine district pride in everyone who attended the Jubilee—if anybody actually came, that is. There were still only seven registrations, a bloody panic situation.

Bobo thought he should put something together for the information booklet. That was great; he could picture his name printed at the foot of each of the stories. Trouble was, when he sat down with a pen in his hand his mind went as blank as the paper in front of him. He couldn't remember anything but vague details about what Rangi told him.

'Are you going to write something or not?' Bobo wanted to know. The people at Crown Press were telling her to hurry up and pull finger about giving them the copy if they wanted the booklet printed on time.

'I'll give them the finger, all right. They've got heaps of time. A hundred and fifty dollars, they're skinning off us.'

'They say they need three weeks clear,' said Bobo, picking at the flaking polish on her long, plum-coloured nails. 'What say I just send in what we've got? People don't want to be lectured at. All they want is a few drinks and a few laughs. This pride in our district idea is boring. I mean, who gives a shit?'

That stung Billy. Of everybody he knew Bobo was the last one he thought would rubbish his ideas. He'd have to prove her wrong too.

Armed with a dozen DB cold ones and a notepad he went to see Rangi Kaawa again.

Though he was more than happy to drink his beer, when Billy pulled out the pad the old man shook his head.

'Kare. No,' he said. 'If you's going to be my mokopuna you's just sit and listen. My stories are like the cobwebs blowing in the wind. You's can breathe on them and watch them sway, but if you's try to grab them, then they disappear.'

So Billy listened, as enraptured as before. Rangi certainly had a way of telling a story to stir the blood. Concentrating so hard, Billy even forgot to drink. When the tray was empty there were only two cans his side and ten on the upturned crate beside the rocking chair.

He hurried home and wrote down as much as he could remember, scribbling far into the night.

Instead of doing the *Herald* crossword at smoko time next day, he read the stories. Disappointment soured his stomach. They sounded so flat and clumsy that he was tempted to chuck the whole idea.

Next morning he took a cup of tea into Pauline. Stooping, he placed the pages on the bedspread beside her as he shook her shoulder.

'*Billy, it's five-thirty!*'

'I know, I know! Look, would you mind glancing at this stuff I've written? See if you can make it more interesting. I mean, I've done all the work — most of it, anyway. All I want you to do is skim over it and change anything you — '

She shut her eyes. 'Billy?'

'What?'

'Do me a favour, huh?'

'Yes, yes. Anything.'

'Bite your bum!'

That afternoon he bailed Lucille up when she was studying in her room. She read the articles doubtfully. 'Gee . . . I never heard none of these stories before, Dad. At school we studied a bit about the history of the district — you know, the Maori wars and stuff — but there was none of this, eh. Nothing about how them local warriors supposedly overran a British fort — '

'Hey, whaddaya mean, "supposedly"? Are you calling Rangi Kaawa a liar?'

'Course not, Dad. Only — '

'Good. Now can you write these out to make them sound more interesting?'

'Don't you think they're interesting enough already?'

'I can do without your sarcasm, girl.'

She pulled a face. 'I'd like to help, but I'm real busy just now.'

He couldn't believe this. 'Too busy to help your old man?'

'It's not that, Dad. I've got these exams on Thursday and Friday, eh. And I'm busy all weekend.'

If the worst came to the worst, he'd have to sacrifice some drinking time. 'Okay. What about Friday night?'

'Sorry. I'm going to the flicks.'

'Not with that boy? Lucille, I've told you — ' Billy saw the glow extinguish from her eyes and didn't have the heart to say what he'd planned. She was so little and so innocent. If there was a boy in her sights it'd only be a girlish crush.

'I'm going with Auntie Minnie,' she said, though she blushed as she spoke. Felipe would be there. Elsie had passed on the message Tuesday lunchtime. Lucille's heart slithered like a car on a wet road just thinking about it.

'You's must be hard up, eh, to look at him,' Elsie had said. 'You's better be quick, too, eh. Dad's going to kill him soon, anyway.'

'What for?'

'Ask him.' Elsie pulled out her chewing gum, looked at it and popped it back in her mouth again. 'Yeah, you ask him. I dare you.'

She'd ask him later. Right now she couldn't help feeling sorry for her father, but she couldn't help, either. 'You don't need me,' she consoled him. 'These stories are really good. Only, if I could suggest making them a bit shorter, eh. People like to read punchy stuff, not stories that ramble on. It's boring when they get like that.'

'Boring?'

'I didn't mean it like *that*.'

Yes she did, he thought gloomily. He was a boring old fart that nobody wanted to help.

He was really on his own this time.

Auntie Minnie smoked all the way into town.

'When are you going to quit, woman? This car smells like a fucking ashtray,' grumbled Potu. 'So does the house. So do all my clothes.'

Mine too, thought Lucille in the back seat. She'd probably wasted that sample of White Gems she'd been given at the Hollingbrook Pharmacy's market day. Felipe would never smell the perfume over the tobacco fumes. At the thought of him sitting close enough to smell her, her body cramped with excitement.

Minnie said, 'The pub smells worse, but that don't stop you going there.' She liked that line. She'd used it a dozen times since Mary Taki came out with it at the meeting that time.

Lucille said, 'I read in the paper that Maori women are five times more likely to get lung cancer than pakeha women.'

'That's bloody racist, that is.'

'No, it's not, Auntie Minnie. They were only trying to warn — '

'It's bloody racist, I tell you.'

Lucille shut up.

Felipe was standing on the edge of the footpath, shiny as the wet road with his slicked-down hair and black leathers. He looked so handsome that Lucille felt dizzy as she climbed out of the car.

'Bloody late, aren't you?' he greeted her. He wasn't used to talking to girls, and Lucille was so beautiful that he felt awkward and inadequate whenever he looked at her.

'Oh, go fuck yourself,' she said, just as if she was one of the guys.

Relaxing, he grinned and flicked his cigarette into the gutter. 'I got us the tickets.'

She rewarded him with a smile that made his hands tremble. 'I'll get us the popcorn, then.'

'See you later, boys and girls,' said Minnie.

In the back row, in the dark, Felipe dropped knobs of popcorn down the front of her low-cut blouse, then fished them out. Lucille's feelings were jumping as if they were in a blender. She was giggling so much that people sitting in the next row told them to shut up.

Felipe kissed her. His mouth was damp and warm and exciting. One of his hands reached up under her skirt. She slapped it away. Felipe didn't mind the slaps. He knew that the thing to do was to keep right on trying. The boys reckoned that petting with a girl was like playing with a kitten — it might scratch you at first but sooner or later pussy would start purring.

Lucille kept her knees jammed together. *I should've worn jeans*, she thought. Tight jeans were the thing, the girls at school reckoned. You had time to argue, time to think, when there were buttons and zips and denim stretched as tight as armour over all your vulnerable bits.

Suddenly she remembered what Elsie had said, about their father killing Felipe. She wondered why. She thought, *If my father could see what he's doing, he'd kill him too.*

Felipe was trying to retrieve a piece of popcorn with his tongue now. 'What's so funny?' he wanted to know.

'Nothing,' she tittered.

'Tell me.'

'Shut up, eh,' said the woman in front. 'You's shut up or I'll box them deaf ears for you, eh.'

She won't talk like that to me soon, thought Felipe. *Not when I'm wearing my patch.*

'Tell me what's so funny,' he insisted as his hand slid under her skirt again.

'It's just that I hope you's got nine lives, eh,' she whispered, shoving it away. 'You just might need them!'

Pauline got a shock on Saturday morning when the Death Raiders came knocking on the door, inquiring after Billy. The leader was a big fellow, with a huge chest and thick arms. He looked even more frightening off his motorbike.

It was not until she saw the look on his face and realised that to him she must look equally shocking, like something from outer space in her paint-covered shirt and shower cap, that she saw the funny side of it. Strange encounters on both sides of her back door.

'He's not here,' she told them. 'He's at the Te Kuiti rugby ground for the day, with the Under Seven Stone tournament. What do you want him for?'

'He's fixing up a job for us, eh.'

'Are you sure it's Billy Williams you want?'

'Yes, ma'am.'

Some of the boys were wandering about the yard. Pauline wondered uneasily if they were sussing the house out for a burglary.

The Mark Three Zephyr captured their attention.

'That's your husband's?'

'It's mine.'

'Been looking for one like that.'

'Have you?' said Pauline. 'Have you, indeed?' She looked at the chaos in the yard. Her blood was fired with zeal. Billy's never would be; she knew that now. 'How much will you give me for it?'

'Aaah, not worth much, eh?'

'How much?'

'Three hundred?'

'Four.'

'Three fifty.'

Pauline nodded. She looked again at the gang members clustered around the car. One of them kept glancing at the house. He looked vaguely familiar.

When Billy came home after the football, tired and smelling of beer, he didn't even notice the great gaping hole in the weeds where the Mark Three used to be. Just as well, thought Pauline. She didn't know how to tell him that the Death Raiders had towed it away with a promise to pay later. He'd go spare when he found out he had to play debt collector to the gang. He'd go even more spare when he found out that she'd agreed on a price of three fifty. He'd paid twelve hundred dollars for the rotten old hulk.

Ten

At three weeks to go there were still only seventeen registrations, and those included the committee members and some of the parents in the district. Frowning, Mr Crawford said not to worry; there was no cause for concern just yet. Mrs Crawford confided to Billy that her husband was worried sick. 'It's vital to his future that the Jubilee is successful,' she said.

As chairman of the committee, and the one who'd lose face if the celebrations flopped, Billy didn't just worry; he panicked. His life had become a twenty-four hour churning mess of apprehension. He couldn't eat because he felt sick. When he forced himself he felt even sicker. Beer tasted rotten, when he had the rare chance to drink some, that was. He couldn't pee to order, not even in the moonlight against the pub wall.

'You's pregnant,' said Honi Fells, shaking his dick and tucking it away.

Potu laughed. He was still in full stream.

Billy said sourly, 'Yeah, I'm pregnant. Pregnant with an idea that's going haywire. How the hell did I get into this?'

'The usual way,' Potu said. 'Somebody fucked you.'

Honi agreed. 'All them fullahs who voted you chairman, they fucked you good.'

'Ha bloody ha,' said Billy gloomily. The Jubilee was shaping up to be a gigantic fiasco. Seventeen people would sit around looking at each other. He should have listened to Potu way back in the beginning. Instead of putting Waimatua on the map he was about to make it a laughing stock.

Even Pauline had no sympathy. 'I told you, it's because everybody is like you — too lazy to send in their registrations. Maybe you need more publicity.'

She could be right for once. She was pasting wallpaper and wouldn't help him, so in desperation he wrote out an ad himself and took it in to the *King Country Gazette*, paying them double rates to run it on the front page, together with an article about what a fine thing Waimatua district was doing, pulling together in such a magnificent cause. Then he hit at grass-roots level, every day after work calling on a different household with the list of jobs to be done for the festivities.

'We tried asking for ordinary volunteers,' he joked. 'Now we're getting army volunteers.' If people looked willing he let them choose a task that took their fancy and wrote their name beside it on the list. If they dithered, he chose for them. 'Think it over,' he urged. 'If you can't do it, come to the next Jubilee Committee meeting on Thursday and tell us there. No worries; we'll find someone else to fill in for you.'

At the same time he got people to fill in their registration forms and took them away, even if the money had to wait until later. Now, at last, he began to feel cautiously confident. Maybe the district would rally round.

His personal worries went by the board in the meantime. He was too busy to think about his money, except for one stray thought when Mrs Crawford started in bleating about having a working bee to raise the rest of the money for the jerseys, so's they could pay off the bill at the store.

Billy stared at her in disgust. Her timing was rotten.

Shit, they'd never worried about paying the jerseys right off in the first weeks of the footie season before. He said, 'I'll see if I can shake any more out of the sponsors,' and wished he hadn't been too mean to fork over the entire amount in the first place. He was getting as tight-arsed as his brother. But before he could go back to the hiding place, other worries intruded and he forgot all about it.

He hadn't spared a thought for the Death Raiders for days. Potu said they'd asked after him at the pub. Not having time to go to the pub every night was a real sore point with Billy, but for a second there he felt glad. He was even too frazzled to think about Bobo, except at meetings when she crossed and uncrossed her luscious, long legs. At those moments he couldn't help thinking about the way he used to find her panties in his pocket, and was glad of the desk screening his lap. What with Pauline being too tired he hadn't had any sex for weeks now, yet committee meetings were the only times that sex penetrated the turmoil in his mind. Maybe he really was sickening for something.

Pauline felt great. 'It's the sense of achievement,' she told Arthur at tea break. 'And nothing seems to bug me these days.' He wondered if she'd noticed the change in her appearance lately. She looked firmer, prettier, with a clear, bold look in her eyes. He lent her some books on self-awareness which she read to and from work on the bus.

Pauline was happy. She ignored the kids' fighting. She ignored Billy, even going to sleep without comment when he woke her with cursed threats to top that squawking rooster. She even stayed calm when she got a phone call from Billy's sister, Nefta, one Thursday night. Miraculously she managed to put a smile in her voice as she greeted her sister-in-law and explained that Billy wasn't home.

Nefta really wanted to speak to Minnie. She'd tried to reach Potu's place but nobody answered the phone. 'She's taken Lucille and Thomas into Taumarunui,' explained Pauline. 'It's their late-night shopping. Minnie and Lucille are choosing some material for party dresses for the big do.'

'I s'pose I'll have to talk to you's instead,' said Nefta ungraciously. Her news was that she and Granny, and maybe some of the rest of her tribe were coming up to stay for the Jubilee.

'That's nice,' said Pauline, though it wasn't.

'Granny keeps harping on about the old place,' whined Nefta's voice along the wires. 'You's know how sentimental she is, eh . . . She wants to know what sort of state it's in.'

Nefta sounded so sly that Pauline had a sudden, horrible premonition. The family down the coast was sick of Granny and her shit-stirring ways. They were anxious to be rid of the old harridan. As clear as if it was happening right before her eyes, Pauline had a vision of Granny settled back next door again, demanding, complaining, causing trouble and spoiling Billy and Potu rotten. She'd made Pauline and Minnie's lives a misery.

'The old house? Oh, it's uninhabitable,' Pauline told her. 'It stinks of damp. There's mildew and rats and holes in the floor — the ceilings, too. Billy's been threatening to pull the whole mess down for ages.'

'You's tell him to wait, okay? We'll camp there for the weekend. We'll look at fixing it up a bit . . . It can't be that bad, can it, eh?'

Pauline sent her love to the family, thanked Nefta again for the whitebait, and assured her that all who wanted to come to the Jubilee would be welcome to stay. As she set the receiver down she smiled as she wondered what the old bag would say about a wife who left her son to cut his own lunch, iron his own clothes or gave him bread and jam for dinner.

Humming to herself she gathered up some newspaper and found a box of matches in the cutlery drawer, then waded through the damp weeds to the old house.

The door creaked open. Inside, the kitchen smelled dry and summery, like good hay. Sunlight filtered through cobwebs on the windows. Pauline dragged the few broken chairs against a wall, piled an old mattress on top and stuffed sheets of crumpled newspaper loosely underneath.

Before she struck a match she wandered through the three tiny rooms, poking in cupboards to make sure nothing of value was left there. All she found were some dented spoons and, under a heap of cushions and magazines in the wardrobe, an old-fashioned blue and white china washbowl and ewer.

The bowl was chipped in two places on the rim. Pauline was going to leave it there but then remembered that she'd seen something similar at the Te Kuiti second-hand mart with a seventy-five dollar price tag. Lumping it outside she set it by the blighted peach tree while she lit the fire.

The newspaper crackled and flames licked a chair leg, which started to burn right away. Pauline carried the bowl and ewer home and got out the hose. Inside the ewer was a wad of jammed-up paper. Nervous of the possibility of mice, Pauline laid the ewer on its side and poked to unplug it with the running hose nozzle.

Just then the fire took hold with a whooshing roar. The noise was tremendous; a hollow, hungry sound clashed through with the clap of exploding windowpanes. Pauline felt a thrill of horrified excitement pass over her body as she gazed at the old shack. Bright flames waved from the windows. The roof seemed to dance in a shimmer of heat. She could feel the tight warm glow of it on her face.

Aware that her shoes were filling with icy water, she looked down. There, washing around her feet in a spreading puddle were *banknotes*. At first she couldn't believe what she was seeing. There were dozens and they had come from inside the ewer: ten dollars, twenties and fifties and lots of dark red hundreds. There must be thousands of dollars here!

'Far out!' she said aloud. 'I've found a bloody fortune!'

The crowd was dispersing by the time Billy came home from his recruiting drive. All that remained was a strong stench of smoke and a glow bruising the ground. The fire had been over so quickly that nobody even bothered to call the fire brigade.

Billy stared at the blackened chimney that stood alone in the scarlet glow. The ground was as flat as if it had been raked over. He felt ill.

My money! he thought.

Pauline dug him in the ribs and jerked her head. Still stunned, he followed her inside and into the bedroom, blinking when she switched the lights on. The new bright-whiteness took a bit of getting used to.

'Look,' she whispered, showing him a damp-looking newspaper that was spread flat on the floor in a corner of the room. She lifted the top layer so that he could see underneath. Side by side, neat as sardines in a tin, were rows and rows of banknotes.

'There's almost five thousand dollars!' she murmured in awe. 'I found it in the old house. I figure it's drug money.' She giggled. 'I accidentally washed it, so it's *laundered* drug money now!'

He wanted to hug her, but at the same time didn't dare let on.

'How do you know it's from drugs?'

'It must be! You know, from when there was that marijuana raid down at the marae a couple of years back? This money was hidden in the old shack, in a hurry, too, I figure. I mean, it was just jammed into that ancient wash-up set. After they hid it the dealers were arrested and sent to prison. That's why they never came back for it.'

Billy's mind raced, but in a dozen different and all equally useless directions. 'They'll come back for it when they're released.'

'They'll see the house is burned down, won't they? They'll think it was an accident — I mean, they'll *know* it was an accident, won't they?'

Billy began to ache to get the money back. It had been a liability for weeks, from time to time he'd even wished that he'd never won the wretched stuff, but now that Pauline was strutting about it being hers he wanted to snatch if off her. It was his, damn it. He *needed* it.

'Give it to me,' he said. 'I'll take it in to the police station — turn it in.'

'No way!'

He felt desperate. He didn't dare confess. She'd murder him if she knew he'd hoarded this for weeks behind her back. 'Give it over, eh? If you don't turn it in, then that's stealing.'

'Stealing from who? The money all came from satisfied customers. They used it to buy dope, sure, but what's the hassle? You've said yourself often enough that you don't think smoking should be a crime. That it's no worse than drinking beer.'

There must be a logical way to prise it out of her grasp, but the best he could come up with was, 'You can't keep it.'

'Oooh! I don't intend to keep it. I've got lots of uses for this, Billy. Lots and lots and lots. That lovely new bedroom suite I've been saving up for, for a start . . . Hey, don't look so upset. You'll get a dip. I'll fix the problem of the football jerseys too. We're having a working bee here on Sunday. Those little buggers on your team can work their tails off cleaning up our yard, digging the garden over, painting the tankstand . . .' She smiled to herself and began to get undressed ready for bed. 'By the way, the fire was my fault,' she continued softly. 'Nefta rang and said that she and Granny and the kids were coming up for the Jubilee and wanted to camp there. I went over to see what state the place was in, and I flicked a few lights on and off. It must have been the wiring that sparked things off. You know, an electrical fault.'

As she spoke she dropped her blouse onto the floor. A box of matches slid out of the pocket. Pauline didn't notice it, but Billy did. He looked at the matches, and then at his wife. She was humming as she snuggled down under the sheets.

Billy frowned. He could have pointed out that there was no way electricity could have started that fire. The power had been disconnected years ago. But for once in his life, Billy said nothing. In the face of her joy he felt miserable. In the face of her confidence he was drained and helpless.

'We should celebrate. Think of it, we're rich!' Pauline reached her arms up to him. Having money was a powerful aphrodisiac. She hadn't felt like this for ages. 'Fancy a cuddle?' she asked coyly.

For once in his life, Billy couldn't respond.

Eleven

'It's my better-late-than-never birthday shout,' explained Pauline as Michael O'Reay sloshed Jim Beam into a plastic jug and topped it up with Coke.

He waved away the proffered money. 'Then, pretty lady, it's a Happy Birthday I'm wishing you.'

'You're in a good mood tonight, Michael.'

He winked at her. 'Ah, yes. There's cause for celebration here, too. Fully booked, we are, and all on account of the Jubilee. That's never once happened in all me time here. I'm after scrubbing all day to get every last inch of the place gleaming like an angel's smile.'

'It always does, Michael.' It was true. The pub was such a credit to him that she sometimes wondered if he was gay. It didn't seem natural for a man to be so enthusiastic about polishing floors and cleaning windows.

'Alas, there's still the wee problem of me courtyard,' he sighed. Pauline Williams had always seemed an insignificant woman to him, but now there was a radiance about her that made him want to confide in her. Before he knew what was happening he was pouring out the woeful tale of men who ignored his pristine urinal in favour of peeing on his walls.

'Jaysus, it's like dogs, they are,' he mourned. 'Like stray, mangy dogs.'

Pauline listened gravely. Her eyes sparkled with mischief.

'Let me tell you what my father does to keep stray mangy dogs off his vegetable garden,' she offered.

Billy still felt resentful because she refused to let go of the money, but at the same time he had to admit that she was handling the responsibility of it well. A few thousand dollars didn't terrify her, and she'd even thought of an excuse for having it — a great-uncle had died and left her a small legacy.

'We have to say something, otherwise we can't spend it. Not in this place where everybody knows everybody's business.'

'You can say that again,' groaned Billy, wishing he'd confided in her at the outset.

Now he sat with Minnie, Potu, Mary Taki, Awhitu Osborne and Honi Fells around half a dozen jugs on the low table. As Pauline rejoined them he said, 'What's all the giggling with O'Reay about?'

'It wasn't "about" anything. At least, nothing that would interest you.'

'Is that bastard O'Reay chatting you up?'

'Don't be silly.' But she was flattered.

'I seen the way he was laughing. Lookit him, he's still bloody killing himself.'

They all looked, at him and then at her.

'If you must know, I was telling him about the electric fence. The one Dad rigged up to keep the dogs away from those prize cabbages in his veggie garden. You remember how that big Labrador came wandering into the yard and limped out on three legs, howling? You thought it was the funniest thing you'd ever seen.'

'Oh... oh, yeah.' But now Billy wasn't really listening. Bobo was sashaying towards him, drop-dead gorgeous as usual in her pink leather jacket, tiny pink mini and black tights. She was waving a huge bundle of letters.

Dropping them in his lap she said, 'Get that, then, eh? Who was worried over nothing, eh? Thirty-three more registrations! That makes seventy-six now, and still a week to go.' She plonked down opposite in a chair Honi had just vacated, and pursed her plum-coloured lips at him. 'That's always been your trouble, hasn't it Billy? Worry, worry, worry over things that never happen.'

He flushed. 'Who me? Not any more.'

'I'll bet. I'll just bet.' She lit a cigarette and blew the smoke through a kiss-shape in his direction.

Minnie scooped up some of the letters and flicked through them, glancing at the return addresses.

'Hey! Lookit this one, you fullahs!' She ripped it open.

'Ace Neville's coming.'

Pauline tried to swallow her mouthful of bourbon and Coke.

'That'll make a stir in the hen-house,' said Potu. 'Great stick-man he was.'

'Ace Neville? No way.' From Honi, who was dragging up another chair.

'Yes he was.'

'Naah. . . You's getting mixed up with Allan. Remember that night he took on the Taumarunui Marching Girls? Shit, that was funny. They could hardly walk afterward, let alone march, eh. Neither could he for that matter, eh. But that's not Ace, the All Black. He was Darcy.'

There was a moment's respectful pause. Then, from Awhitu, 'Yeah. Ace was always serious. Quiet, eh. Until he got onto a rugby field. He was a devil then.'

'Wonder if he'll put on a goal-kicking demo for the Under Seven Stones?' wondered Billy.

'Nah, no chance,' said Minnie. 'Them doctors, they made him give it away when he had that accident — you's remember — five years ago, eh? Smashed his leg ... Just about crippled him for life. Poor bloody sod. He was one of the finest All Blacks we've ever seen.'

There was a moment's silence.

'Smashed up his marriage, too,' mused Bobo who knew of the legendary Ace Neville through the gossip columns of which she was an avid reader. 'His wife left him for the captain of the Australian team right after that happened.'

Awhitu swigged at his beer. He grinned like a baby, showing all his pink gums. 'Goes to show, eh, that there's a bright side to everything.'

'That's a rotten thing to say!' declared Mary Taki.

'No it ain't. I knew her well, don't you fullahs forget that. Isobel Flanders was a rotten, stuck-up bitch. Dunno why Ace ever married her.'

Honi laughed. 'Don't you's remember? Hey, it was the joke of the year when he came unstuck.' He grinned around the table. 'She was the team manager's daughter, that's why. She chased after him, hung about like a bad smell, and then got him at some after-match function in Feilding or somewhere. She was pregnant right off. Course he married her. Nobody puts the team manager's daughter up the stick and gets away with it.'

Feeling ill, Pauline pushed back her chair. Nobody noticed her leave.

Lucille lay on her bed reading *Dolly* magazine while Prince blasted full-volume on the stereo.

She was fretting. Why hadn't Felipe asked her to the

movies again? He'd promised that he'd see her again Saturday, and here it was, nine o'clock and there had been nothing. No message from Elsie, no phone call.

He'd seemed keen, but maybe that was all an act. Maybe he was disappointed in her. Maybe she should have let him go just a little bit further. If only she knew what to do!

Maybe his father had killed him after all, as Elsie said he would. She was still in the dark about that, too.

She was reliving their last kiss and feeling achey inside when the motorbikes arrived. The grumbling roar wiped out the noise of Prince, full blast on the stereo. When she looked out the window she saw a dozen Death Raiders swaggering up the path. That gave her a shock.

She got an even bigger shock when she saw Felipe tagging behind them. He looked different, too. In Lucille's mind Felipe had always been a big, macho guy. Now he seemed shrunken and timid. Lucille felt too scared to move.

Pauline walked up the road just as the motorbikes turned into her driveway and cut their lights. Remembering that Lucille was home alone she broke into a run and, by cutting across the grass, reached the steps at the same moment as the leader. He was bulkier than she remembered, looming in the dark in a way that couldn't help but seem menacing, and he smelled like old, unwashed clothes.

She was about to blurt, 'What are you doing here? What do you want?' but in time remembered something from one of Arthur Nimwood's books.

She looked him straight in the eye. 'Good evening,' she panted as pleasantly as she could. 'I suppose you've come to pay me for the car? That's very decent of you to be so prompt. It was three hundred and fifty dollars we agreed on, wasn't it?' And she held out her hand.

'What did you mean by that crack?' asked Billy.

'What crack?'

'You know damned well.'

'No I don't.'

It was later that same night. They were in Billy's ute, outside Bobo's place. The babysitter was peeking through the curtains of the lounge.

'Yes you do. That crack about how I'm always worrying about things that never happen.'

Bobo laughed. She had never been turned on by Cliff Richard — he was too soft-looking for her — but there was no getting away from it: Billy was easily the sexiest man in the district. She leaned over and kissed him full on the mouth, probing his lips with her tongue.

Her laugh annoyed him. Despite the tobacco taste her kiss was unbearably exciting. That annoyed him even more. 'Why don't you give up smoking?' he griped.

Her hand slid down to his lap. She laughed again, this time at what her fingers encountered. It was so impressive that she fluttered as she said, 'Why don't you give up thinking about me?'

'Because I can't bloody help it.'

'How tough life is,' she said, opening the door.

He grabbed at her and missed. She slipped away, fading into the darkness as quickly as the mocking laughter that trailed like perfume behind her.

Paulie was sitting up in their new bed, on a new, comfortable mattress with new, soft pillows at her back, as she read *Assertiveness is the Answer*. She looked over the tops of her glasses as Billy came in. As he unbuttoned his shirt his face was reflected in the new oval mirror. She pretended not to watch as he surreptitiously wiped lipstick traces off his lower lip.

'Why'd you run off and leave us like that?'

'No reason.' She could hardly admit that it hurt to hear gossip about Darcy. 'Just as well that I did. Those gang friends of yours were here when I got home.'

He said nothing as she turned a page, though she hadn't finished reading it. 'Mrs Crawford left a message with Lucille. The donated groceries are ready. She wants to know if you can run in to Te Kuiti to collect them tomorrow. They'll have to be distributed as soon as possible.'

Damn. He'd forgotten all about the groceries. 'I'll round up some of the team to help first thing.'

'No you won't. We're having a working bee — remember?'

'Surely you don't need the whole team to — '

'Yes I do. Besides, if some come with you the others will sulk and I'll get no work out of any of them.'

'Aw, come on.'

'No, I won't come on. I need them all, and that's that.'

'It's not like you to be selfish.'

'*Selfish?*' Everything erupted inside her. Her having to take over Billy's job of cleaning the yard. His shrew of a mother arriving to stay any day. The gang being here and scaring poor Lucille half to death. Billy's accusations of selfishness were the last straw.

'I'm selfish, am I?' she said coldly. 'What about you, coming home festooned with *Mrs Penny's* lipstick?'

'You're imagining things.'

'Okay, I'm imagining things.' She was too plain fed-up to care anyway. 'A word of advice, eh? When you eat blackberry iceblocks, or whatever put that stain on your face, you might try to be a bit tidier about it.'

Cheeky bitch! If she'd put the light out and settled down to sleep Billy would have approached and kidded her around under the pretext of making up the quarrel. His balls were aching with the worst frustration in living memory, and she looked pretty in that new ruffled nightie with the low cleavage. But instead of settling down, she pushed her glasses back up her nose and continued reading her book. When he reached out to touch her she shrugged him off.

'Ah, come on, Paulie. We haven't christened our new bed yet.'

'I'm not in the mood,' she said.

He had a sudden, horrid thought. 'Hey, you're not turning into a women's libber, are you?'

Pausing for a moment to consider, she shook her head. 'No. I'm just growing a little, that's all.' He was beginning to relax when she added, 'You might like to try it yourself. You've never really grown up, have you?'

Bitch!

In their bedroom in the house next door Potu was speculating about Billy driving off with Bobo after they left the pub. He felt faintly jealous — Bobo was so gorgeous that a man would have to be made of stone not to feel some twinge of envy — but Potu was concerned, too.

'Nah, no worries,' said Minnie, unsnapping a suspender and rolling a stocking down over her gigantic thigh. 'Billy's got more sense than to have another set-to with Jim.'

'Billy's like anybody else, eh. Sometimes he's sensible

and sometimes he's a stupid fucking idiot,' said Potu.

'Naah. Besides, that silly business was over years ago.'

'Silly Billy business is never over, eh.' He made a growling noise. The sight of black lace and Minnie's gigantic thighs did something powerful to him.

He lunged.

'Get off me, you's great useless raho!' But she giggled and cut him a sly look.

He lunged again. Minnie could stand a lot of lunging. Especially when she was in one of her coy moods.

Like now.

Twelve

Next morning it was Billy who was in a mood. A foul one. Half a dozen of his Under Seven Stones were already out in the yard, dragging rubbish out of the shed, pulling weeds in the garden, hammering loose fence palings back into place. Those bloody chooks were going crazy, cackling and crowing.

Thomas was up a ladder scooping leaves out of the guttering. In overalls and a headscarf, Pauline stirred paint as she supervised.

Lucille cooked Billy's breakfast. When she put the plate of bacon and eggs in front of him he said, 'I don't suppose these eggs are from those useless birds of yours, are they?'

'Grumpy, Dopey . . . and . . . and Doc are too young to lay yet.'

'But not too young to wake the district. If they're roosters, they're for the chop, you know that, don't you?'

To his amazement she burst into tears.

'Hey!' he said alarmed. 'Princess, don't take it to heart. They're only chooks after all — '

She slammed out of the room.

He couldn't do anything right, it seemed.

It was a beautiful day. By the time Billy had loaded up the back of the ute the sunshine had warmed his soul, evaporating the last of his sour spirits. He was reaching under a carton of toilet rolls for the tarp to cover everything when Abe Langley saw him from the upstairs window of Crown Press. He shouted, and beckoned Billy over.

'What are you doing, working on a Sunday?'

'Had a spot of trouble with the machines throwing a wobbly yesterday. All okay now. But look, here's the first of your souvenir programmes. It's not stapled yet, but it looks good, don't you think?'

With a feeling of awe Billy took the purple-covered booklet. The jacket wore Billy's own line drawing of hills, a stream and a clump of cabbage trees above the legend: WAIMATUA — THE SOURCE.

'You're pleased then?'

'It looks great . . . really great.' Billy flicked through and found the first of Rangi Kaawa's pieces, the one about how Te Rauparaha was so impressed by the bravery of one of his warriors that he named him Te Waimatua, in this case meaning the source of his determination to conquer. It looked so stirring in print that reading it through, Billy felt a ridiculous grin spreading over his face.

'What did you's think of it?'

'Whoever put it together did a good job. Some of those stories are a bit of a dag, too.'

Before Billy could ask what he meant by that, Abe said, 'I've taken the liberty of using that cover design for a logo on some tee shirts.' He disappeared into the back room and came back with a white shirt, a black and a red one each with the hills and river and WAIMATUA, 100 YEARS — I RETURNED TO THE SOURCE printed neatly where a breast pocket might be.

'I thought you could display these at the registration counter and maybe take orders from anybody who wants to buy one,' Abe explained.

Billy wished he'd thought of the idea first. He promptly ordered a dozen for his helpers to wear over the weekend and left with the three samples and the booklet.

A crowd of kids were playing around the ute. They jumped off the back and scampered quickly away when Billy yelled at them. He then climbed into the ute and drove home.

Pauline's working bee were out in front of the house, trimming the path, painting the steps and mowing the grass verge. Billy didn't recognise the back yard — it was so flat and bare and tidy it was more like something you'd expect to see in town. Where was the Mark Three? he wondered, as the boys came racing towards the ute, scattering Lucille's chooks in a flurry of squawks.

Billy thought that the team were cheering to see him, then realised they were shrieking with laughter. When he stopped and climbed out, he realised why.

Dragging in the road behind him were metres and metres of unwound tissue trailing like the threads of some gigantic white jellyfish. Every bog roll in the box had been unwound and left to play out in the wind.

Billy remembered the children who'd been playing on the back.

'Those bloody kids!' he said.

He left some of the streamers floating while he delivered the flour and sugar around to the women who'd agreed to cook. The women all reacted to the grocery contribution in a slightly different way.

'You's didn't need to bring the ingredients,' protested Mary Taki. 'I told you's fullahs that I'm only too glad to whip up a few batches of scones. It's all in a good cause, eh?'

'Get outa here with that stuff,' insisted Aramoana Kingi. She pushed him and his grocery carton out the door.

Titewhai, Rangi Kaawa's daughter, was even more insistent that he take the supplies away. 'I'm down for a dozen sponge rolls, and I already bought all the stuff, enough to make one-and-a-half dozen big ones. The good stuff, too. None of this donated rubbish, eh.'

'If we don't use it, then you fullahs can raffle it, eh,' said Irene Wilkinson from up the valley. She poured him a cup of tea and nudged a plate of fresh date scones towards him.

Jessie Morrison checked her supplies off against a check-list on her Leave-A-Note. 'I hope the eggs will be provided too,' she reminded him. 'We're prepared to make the pikelets and use our power, but as Janey said, the Jubilee is a commercial venture after all.'

As he went he proudly flashed the tee shirts and the souvenir programme. The shirts were a great hit; people exclaimed over them and wanted to buy them. Billy was disappointed that the book didn't stir similar enthusiasm.

'Unlettered peasants,' he muttered.

He particularly wanted to show the programme off to Rangi Kaawa, but he wasn't home.

'Sorry,' Titewhai said as she followed him and his groceries back out to the ute. 'It's this bloody asthma, eh. His grandson he took him to the doctor. What say you's give me the book so's I can show it to him when he comes back.'

Billy pictured how it might look after Titewhai's tribe had all raked their grimy fingers over the cover and thumbed the new white pages. 'Aaah, I'll bring it back, eh.'

The packages containing the marquee were so large that the load wouldn't even look at the back of Billy's ute. Billy rang the schoolhouse.

'Are you sure you can't manage it?' carped Mr Crawford. 'Hiring a truck means extra cost, you know, and all those ads of yours have already blown the budget sky-high.'

Billy struggled for control. 'If you're worried about the money then perhaps you could put rollers under it and have all the schoolchildren tow it along the road, like the ancient Egyptians did when they built the pyramids. If you's get organised now, they'd be at the school by next Tuesday, eh. But seriously, I suggest that you's ring the truckies now, eh. Me, I need a drink.' And hanging up, he strode across the road to the Te Kuiti Tavern.

Delivered to the school grounds next afternoon, the marquee made two shed-sized humps on the playground.

'You fullahs got the instructions?' asked Honi.

Awhitu was struggling with the knots in the laced-up rope of one hump. 'You's don't need instructions. I seen one go up in five minutes. In one of them Elvis movies, eh. Piece-a-cake. No worries, not with us keen types.'

'Dunno,' said Potu. 'Might be a job for the experts, eh.'

Privately, Billy suspected that he might be right. There was so much *more* of it than he'd imagined. He doubted, too, that a half-remembered Elvis movie would provide much practical instruction.

'No papers in here,' reported Awhitu.

'What we gonna do, eh?'

'Maybe we should get Mr Crawford.'

'Whadda we need him for?'

'He arranged the bloody thing. Let him work it out, eh.'

While they all argued the toss, nothing was getting done. Billy was exasperated. 'I heard that there's half a dozen trays of DB under that marquee. You fullahs better find them, before they get warm.'

It couldn't be that difficult if it needed no special instructions, Billy reasoned. Assuring them all that this would be the same as putting up a regular tent, only on a slightly bigger scale, Billy proceeded with confidence. They spread the canvas sections out, admiring the pretty red and green colours. They found the circumference poles and assembled the main supports for the roof. It was then that things became confused. The marquee now extended over half the football field but it was flat on the ground. They had no real idea of what to do next.

When Potu again suggested that they see if Mr Crawford had received some instructions when he ordered the thing, Billy was ready to agree.

Decidedly frosty when she saw Billy at the door, Mrs Crawford explained that her husband had gone into town. Potu persuaded her to look in his desk for anything from the hire people. After taking enough time to search the whole house she came back to the door with a letter from Citywide Marquee Hire.

'Is this any help?' She held it out to Potu but Billy snatched it, read the letter and handed it back.

'What did it say?' From Potu as Billy stamped down the path to the ute.

Billy gunned the motor. 'It said that Mr Crawford saved us five hundred dollars on that marquee. We thought he was a real clever bloke. Only trouble is, the five hundred dollars was the cost of having someone come down and put it up for us. That tight-arsed bastard.'

'If we think it's too difficult for us to figure out, then maybe we should leave it until he comes back, eh,' suggested Potu slyly.

He knew Billy would rise to the challenge, and he did. 'Stuff that! We're not beaten yet, bro.'

He felt differently when it was getting dark. The mess on the football field looked more confusing by the minute. All they'd figured out was where all the separate main pieces belonged. How they fitted together and in what order remained anybody's guess. Everybody was giving orders, but because none of the orders made much sense, nobody was taking any notice. Billy felt like bawling. He felt like strangling Mr Crawford. He also felt determined. There had to be some straightforward way to fit the puzzle together.

A cluster of children had arrived to watch. Lucille was there too. Thomas and some of the other boys burrowed under the canvas, shrieking, until Honi roared at them to go away.

Billy stood on the back of the ute, fists jammed in his pockets. *How?* he thought furiously. For the first time in the six years since he'd given the weed away, he'd have murdered for a fag. Potu came over. 'Maybe if we rang those fullahs in Auckland, eh, asked them to send someone down urgently — '

Billy shook his head. 'No! We can do it, I know we can.' He stared at the pieces, then grinned as an answer came to him. It was a magical moment, as if a weight slid from his mind. 'I know what to do! I remember that movie now. We tie the tops of the poles to a rope, then have the ute *tow* it upright.'

That seemed logical. Talking excitedly they cut out a plug of turf to make a hole for the base of the first pole, then Honi and Awhitu stood ready to steady the base into place while Potu roped in Lucille and some of the bigger children to hold the wires out at the sides, well back out of the way.

When everything was in place, Billy eased the ute into low gear and let it crawl across the grass. Supervising, Potu shouted instructions.

In the rear-vision mirror Billy saw the pole rise metre by metre against the darkening sky. His spirits rose right along with the pole. When Potu yelled at him to stop he cut the motor and climbed out of the cab, gazing up in pride.

But something was wrong. It had to be an optical illusion, the way the pole was swaying, thought Billy, but no sooner had he decided that, than he realised it was no illusion at all. The pole was falling, and he was right in its path. Lucille was screaming something at him; he couldn't hear what. He stood, gaping at the pole. It fell so slowly that it seemed to grow thicker and thicker and as it came down it whistled.

It's going to kill me! thought Billy, breaking into a run. The pole hit down behind him with a force that made the ground shudder. When he turned, Billy saw that it had missed the ute by less than half a metre.

Lucille was running towards him. 'Dad, are you all right?'

'Never better.' Though it was a lie. His legs were weak as drinking straws under him; he felt useless and stupid and angry.

'Us fullahs balls'd that up, eh?' grinned Awhitu, chuffed that Billy's ute hadn't copped it. That pole had whacked down like a fly swat landing on a fly. The ute would've been history.

Standing on the tray to survey the damage, Billy despaired. They'd balls'd it up, all right. Furthermore, word of this would get out and the whole of the King Country would be wetting themselves over the poor sods from Waimatua — so thick that they couldn't even put up a little tent without screaming for help. *What do you call 144 Waimatua men?* (Gross ignorance.) *What do you call a Waimatua pup tent?* (An insurmountable challenge.) He could hear the laughter already, and he squirmed in humiliation. 'Bum titty fart!' he bellowed. He pounded on the roof of the ute and kicked his boots against the sides of the tray, cursing at the top of his lungs.

He was shouting so loudly that he didn't hear the bikes come blatting up the road. They turned into the school gate and, like a flock of big, black bugs swarmed idly across the football field.

'Hey, mate!' called Larry. 'You got a problem here, I think.'

'Just a little setback, eh,' admitted Potu. 'Nothing that we can't sort out by — '

Ignoring him, Larry addressed himself to Billy. 'If you've got a problem, then I think we just got ourselves a job.'

The leader swung off his bike, climbed up onto the ute beside him, raked his thick fingers through the sides of his hair and stared at the marquee. In bits and pieces it lay around the field, red and green and tangled like so much spaghetti and salad. *He's come to laugh*, Billy guessed, gazing at the gang leader in distaste. *Well I might as well get used to it. Everybody's going to be laughing soon.*

Larry said, 'To begin with, you haven't got the king poles — that's those big ones — fitted into the base plates.'

'Base plates?'

'Those metal things over there, they're the base plates. See? They hold the king poles upright. You had the right idea using the ute, but the bellrings with the clamps in place should have been attached to the guide wires first, and that winch should be fitted onto the king pole so that once she's standing up the roof sections can be hauled into their right positions.'

Billy gaped at him.

'Have you measured up? For this size marquee, the king poles should be exactly ten metres apart. The roof sections won't fit, otherwise.'

Billy was still gaping.

The leader grinned, showing large, yellow teeth. He spat over the side of the ute, narrowly missing Potu who was gaping up at him too.

'I used to be a roustabout with the circus,' he said, vaulting down. 'Come on lads. Let's see how long it takes us to get this show on the road.'

It took sixteen and a half minutes.

Thirteen

While Billy was narrowly escaping death under the king pole, Minnie picked Pauline up from her after-work appointment at the hairdresser and took her to meet Granny and Nefta off the bus. The bus was early; they were late. Granny and Nefta were waiting on the pavement surrounded by bundles and flax kits and cardboard cartons tied up with baling twine.

'Where's the kids?' asked Minnie.

'Good to see you, too,' snipped Nefta. She looked like a bad-tempered version of Potu, but much fatter and with lots of thick, grey hair that was loose around the fur collar of her coat. More hair sprouted from moles on her chin and left cheek.

'Aaah, give over, eh. Where are they?'

Granny was piqued at being ignored. She was as small as a seven-year-old, with a child's shrill voice. Her face and neck were wrinkled like a tortoise's. 'They got better things to do than hang around with us old things,' she said. Then, when Minnie kissed her: 'Hmph! Given up dieting, I see.'

Minnie giggled. She was always good at handling Granny. 'But not smoking, Granny. I haven't gone that far.'

'Glad to hear that, girlie. I can bludge one now, then, can't I, eh?'

Neither she nor Nefta kissed Pauline. Being pakeha she was not one of them, a judgment Pauline had always thought hilarious, for Granny was at least half pakeha herself.

Both Granny and Nefta took in Pauline's red leather jacket, knee-length matching skirt, elegant red shoes and red spotted stockings. Both noted her smartly styled hair.

'Hmph,' said Granny.

'And how are you then, Pauline?'

'Fine thank you Nefta. How are you?'

'Fine, just fine.'

'Did you have a good trip?'

'Yes, thank you.'

'How's the family?'

'Fine, thank you.'

'What about you, Granny? How are you?'

'So she's noticed me! And whaddaya think you's doing, eh Pauline, gadding about dressed up like that? Don't you's think those kinds of clothes is for young ones?'

'No, Granny, I don't. And furthermore, what I wear is my business. *That's* what I think.'

They all stared at her.

Larry said, 'Yeah. Spent five years travelling back and forth across Australia with the Aztec Brothers' Circus. Got thrown out in the end for fucking the elephant.'

Billy slopped beer all over the table.

'The *elephant?* No sweat?' from Honi.

'Plenty sweat, as it happens.' During the laughter Michael O'Reay came scurrying over with a cloth and sopped up the spill. His prim face was a study in disapproval.

When he had retreated Larry continued, 'But not a real elephant, you understand. The owner's wife, she were. Twenty stone of deep heaven, I tell you. Great billowing armfuls of baby-powdered flesh. Earned her

keep as the fat lady.' He lowered his voice. 'Best ride I
ever had, too. You wanna try it sometime. First of all
screw your average pin-up type woman, then try one of
these big mommas. I mean, *real* big. There ain't no
comparison, mate. You can keep your centrefold sheilas,
no worries. Them big mommas is heaven on earth.'

Huge Hemi and toothless Awhitu tried to look as if
they might someday have the opportunity to try this
experiment.

Potu nodded sagely. Being married to Minnie, he
understood the truth in what was being said.

Understanding too, Billy winked at his brother. He
wondered why he'd ever been scared of such a great
bunch of guys.

'Hey, why you being snobby with me?'

Lucille walked faster. The others had gone, roaring
off to the pub. Thomas and the other children ran
shrieking after the bikes.

Felipe caught up to Lucille and grabbed her arm. She
was still so disappointed in him that her body shuddered
as she shook herself free. 'Fuck off.'

'No way.' He grabbed her again.

She whirled to face him. Through the dusk she could
see the hurt in his eyes.

'Oh, Felipe.'

'What'samatter, eh? Why you's gone cold on me,
girl?'

'It's not you. It's the gang.'

'Oh.' Not knowing what else to be, he acted defensive.
He was good at that. It came of practice. 'What'samatter
with the gang?'

'How can you even *ask*?'

She sounded so defeated that he let go of her. Shit,

she had that sick gearbox whine like his old lady. But watching her walk away made him panic. She was only a few metres up the road when he decided to run after her again.

She was plugged with rage, choking on it. 'Why'd you go and join a *gang*?'

He sighed.

'Why?' She stamped her foot at him. Like one of those pretty calves with great dark eyes, he thought.

'Hey, you's listen to me, at least, okay?' He took her hand and this time she didn't pull away. 'You's don't know what it's like for me, eh. Listen, okay?'

'Okay. I'll listen.'

They sat side by side on an old tractor tyre which lay on the roadside verge outside the Fells' woolshed. The centre had been filled with soil and planted with flowers during Mrs Crawford's 'beautify the district' binge, but the flowers died and the soil had long ago washed away, leaving only the ugly tyre.

While the darkness deepened around them, Felipe told her about his life. How each morning he and Denis trudged around town asking if there was any work, and how in the afternoon they had nothing to do but sit in the park, talking and smoking, just kicking time along to make it go faster.

'Nobody wants us, eh. There's no jobs anywhere and 'cos we's on the dole, everybody they think we's useless, we's layabouts. D'you know how that feels, having nothing to do?'

'I'd have thought it felt like being on holiday.'

'Holiday? Hah! Yeah, maybe it did for the first coupla weeks after I got chucked out of school, but then it's like in the movies when those walls tighten in to squash you's. You's trapped, eh. You's feel hopeless,

112

like nothing you's do is going to fix it, no matter how you struggle. And then it gets worse until you's don't even want to do anything, eh. You's don't want to get out of bed in the morning. That's the worst part, eh. When you wake up and think about how you's got this day in front of you, and it might be sunny, eh, or it might be rainy, but you's just don't want to know.'

Lucille's eyes were luminous in the dusk. She put a hand on his arm but said nothing.

'I know you's think the gangs are shit. Everybody thinks that, but let me tell you's this, eh, shit where nobody wants you's is the pits to the max — fucking miles worse than shit where somebody says hi, and hey bro, and all that stuff. When Larry, he said maybe we might like to join the gang, it weren't no dream come true. My folks went ape-shit, and even I don't feel so flash about it. But those guys are staunch. They's mates.'

Lucille was wavering. The despair in Felipe's voice shocked her; she hadn't realised how tough the world was for young men without jobs.

'But couldn't you get other mates? I mean, those guys are *criminals*!'

'Who ain't, huh? What's a criminal anyway, eh? You name me one person who ain't told lies or cheated, or smoked grass, or pinched from the boss, or worked an' collected a benefit or got a bit extra on the side. Name me one, huh?'

Lucille thought hard. Auntie Minnie told Uncle Potu fibs all the time, and her father had been sinful with Mrs Penny. Thomas was as dishonest as the devil himself.

'Come on. Betcha you don't know nobody who never cheated on anybody, huh?'

'My mother,' said Lucille. 'So there!'

Minnie bought a big bundle of fish and chips while Pauline stocked up on extra milk and bread at the dairy. When they got home they spread out the food on the new, blue Formica table in Pauline's smart blue and white kitchen.

Neither Granny nor Nefta complimented Pauline on how pretty the house looked. Granny ate as if she was doing them a favour. 'Not a patch on our fish and chips down the coast, eh Nefta?'

Nefta was hoeing in greedily. She started to agree then switched tack. 'Nah, Granny, you's just tired, eh.' To Minnie she said, 'You should hear her. Always harping on about how good the kai is in Te Kuiti.'

'I never done that!'

'Course you's do. Always, Te Kuiti this and Waimatua that. We's never been good enough for you. You's always harping back to the happy days, eh. The happy days here.' In case anybody missed the point, she added, 'Funny, eh, how old peoples is always wanting to go back where their roots are.'

Pauline got up to make a pot of tea. She smiled at her reflection in the dark window. She could feel good about this visit, she could even feel great, because she knew that very soon Nefta and Granny would go away again . . . because they had to.

'Pity about the old house burning down,' she said.

She was in such a good mood that when Billy brought the nametags in to be finished off, instead of telling him to get lost Pauline agreed to help.

'Thanks,' he said, relieved. The excitement was winding in huge hard coils inside him. 'We've still got the chairs and tables to set out. Bobo was going to do this, but she's had to drive up to Te Kuiti to collect the decorations. They were supposed to come today, but they're still at the rural delivery depot.'

So while Granny and Nefta and Thomas watched Arnold Schwartzenegger videos at Minnie's place, Minnie, Lucille, and Pauline worked in the blue and white kitchen sticking stars on the nametags. They worked fast, checking each tag against Bobo's neat list in the register.

The stars were in various colours and proclaimed what the wearer had paid for and was therefore entitled to attend. There was a red star for Friday night's wine and cheese, blue star for morning and afternoon teas, a silver star for lunch, a gold star for the big banquet, and a green star for the hangi on Sunday. So far they had forty-eight red stars, a hundred and twenty blue and silver stars, a hundred and five gold stars and ninety green stars.

Darcy Neville had registered for everything.

Minnie collected Pauline from work on Friday and together they shopped for cheese, crackers, cheerios, nuts and pâté from the supermarket, then went to the pub for the wine casks, plastic glasses and containers of fruit juice.

At the school Bobo and Mary Taki were already arranging the senior classroom for the wine and cheese. The children had worked all week putting up festive decorations. Purple and red crêpe paper streamers sagged below the ceiling. Hand-drawn posters depicting scenes from the past covered the walls. The blackboard had been cleaned and washed, then decorated in coloured chalk with the legend: WELLCOME TO THE WAIMATUA SCHOOL JUBILEE.

The young Taki boys carried the chairs and half of

115

the desks out into the next room, then shoved the remaining desks together in the centre of the floor space to make a single long table. Bobo and Mary spread first bedsheets then lace tablecloths over this table. Two of Bobo's floral arrangements, roses and trailing jasmine, graced the centre of the table. It looked beautiful, if out of place in a classroom.

'Like a wedding,' approved Bobo.

When Pauline and Minnie arrived the four women worked fast, cutting cheese, setting out biscuits and pâté and shooing the boys away.

'Tomato sauce!' cried Bobo. 'There's no sauce!'

'Oh, dear. We forgot all about it,' said Pauline.

Minnie had a new bottle at home. 'No worries. Can't have those fullahs going spare at us, can we. Cheerios ain't the same without tomato sauce.'

'The cheerios! They need heating.' Bobo was flushed with excitement. In less than two hours the Jubilee would be under way.

'Don't panic, eh.' From Minnie.

Pauline stared at the blackboard. 'Welcome has only one "L", hasn't it?' she said.

Minnie took the cheerios home to heat up in her big soup pot. Bobo fixed the blackboard.

In her new bedroom with the green-sprigged curtains Pauline dressed in her red outfit. She bent over at the waist to brush her hair downwards, then sprayed it with hairspray to make it stay fluffed out. Her breathing was ragged. She made such a mess of her eye makeup that she had to coldcream her face and start all over again.

She felt icy inside. She wondered about running away. Above everything else, she wished she was somewhere else. *Mark this one, girl,* she told her reflection.

You're tashed and you're past it and if Darcy Neville looks at you at all, it's going to be with pity.

She knew that Arthur Nimwood would disapprove if he knew how defeated she was feeling right now. She didn't care. Glumly she checked the wrinkles under her chin and around her eyes.

They were still there.

Fourteen

'Is that you, Lucille?' called Pauline.

'Sorry I'm late, Mum. I had . . . a few things to do in town after school.'

'Until this hour?'

'I said I'm sorry!'

'Well you'd better hurry up. We're late already.'

Lucille was going to waitress. On her bed was a black dress with a frilly white lace pinny that Minnie made especially.

Lucille ran water into the handbasin, wrung out a facecloth and pressed it against her neck. She felt hot and happy, as if something pleasant was swelling inside her. When she took the facecloth away and looked in the mirror, she saw the three lovebites on her neck. They looked like badges. 'Promises,' said Lucille. She was not a woman yet, but she soon would be.

She took her mother's pancake makeup out of the cupboard above the basin, moistened the sponge and began cover-up operations.

Billy was drunk. He and Potu stopped by the pub for a quick one after work and the gang were there. Five minutes turned into an hour, then two. Now, outside, he could hardly stand up straight as he pissed against the wall. He was giggling so loudly it was a wonder Michael O'Reay didn't hear.

Potu drove the ute home so's they could get poshed up for the wine and cheese. Billy sprawled against the door.

'Fucking the elephant! What a bloody dag, eh?'

While Potu had been as amused as anyone yesterday, Billy's harping made it less and less funny. Annoyed, he told Billy to can it.

Billy didn't take any notice; he still thought it was the best joke he'd ever heard. 'Fucking the elephant!' he kept saying. They lurched to a stop in Billy's driveway. Potu reached across his brother. 'Why don't you shut up, eh, bro,' he said, and opened the door suddenly so that Billy fell out backwards into a newly planted flowerbed.

'Whaddayou do that for?'

'To knock some sense into you's silly head, *mate*!'

The senior room was crowded. Women eyed each other surreptitiously. Men looked ill at ease in jackets and ties. Smokers hung onto their ciggies, puffing nervously. Between the streamers and the ceiling smoke was stuffed as thick as insulating batts. Rangi Kaawa held court next to the open doorway. In between phrases he sipped little breaths of fresh air. He wore his rug around his shoulders.

Mrs Crawford shot Pauline and Minnie a 'where have you been?' look. Also positioned by the door, she welcomed guests and handed them their name tags and Jubilee books from the array displayed on the desk in front of her.

Pauline apologised for being late. She promised to take over as soon as she'd had a wine. Her voice came out in a squeak first time, so she had to repeat herself. Within three seconds of stepping into the room she'd sussed that Darcy hadn't arrived yet.

They were spoiled for choice, she decided as she tried to choose between the large cardboard casks of

Chablis, Müller Thurgau, Moselle and Sauterne. It would have been nice to be really posh and have the wine in bottles, she thought as she filled a plastic-stemmed glass. Mr Crawford nixed that idea, of course, on account of the budget.

Granny downed three brimming juice tumblers of Sauterne in swift succession, then opened her souvenir book. Because it was always her policy to wait for others to come to her, she ignored the people in the room and began to read. Her lips moved as she read.

Nefta sipped through pleated lips. She said, 'I hate wine. Gizza beer any day.'

'We considered having beer, eh, but thought it's be too much of a booze-up,' Minnie told her.

'So this is s'posed to be posh?' sniffed Nefta. She kept still, with only her eyes shifting constantly, like a praying mantis does when watching for insects.

Minnie whispered to Pauline that Nefta had come to the Jubilee with the hopes of catching another man. With many of her old schoolmates and ex-boyfriends here, she would have plenty to choose from, she reckoned.

'Only if they don't mind whiskers,' said Pauline absently. There was no sign of Ace Neville.

Minnie giggled. Neither of them liked Nefta.

Perhaps he isn't coming after all, hoped Pauline.

Billy and Potu arrived, both looking dishevelled and talking loudly. Minnie hurried over to them. She took Potu's elbow and drew him aside. His breath reeked of beer.

'Whaddaya go and get sozzled for? Billy's got to give a speech and lookit him! Jeez, can't you's do anything right?'

Potu smiled loosely and reached out his hands. Her breasts were as full and soft as sofa cushions. Under that silk blouse were big, black nipples like soft-centred chocolates. Drunk as he was, his lust stirred.

Lovely Minnie; Larry was right. You could keep your scrawny centrefolds.

Furious, Minnie slapped his hands away. 'I need your help.'

'You got it, babe!'

She backed away. 'Jeez-zus! The only time you's want to do anything it's when you's can take off your bloody trousers! Behave yourself, okay?'

He leered, still grabbing.

People around them were staring. Mary Taki thought it was a huge joke. Armed with fresh — and practical — knowledge in the ways of sex, Lucille imagined that she was witnessing the start of a public seduction. Alarmed, she hovered with a tray laden with cheese and biscuits, then thrust it between them. 'Have something to eat?'

Bobo said, 'I've never seen Billy so wiped out.'

'It's nerves,' Pauline told her. She'd kill him when she got home. Nah, why bother? He'd kill himself when he realised he'd stuffed up his big moment.

Darcy Neville's name card was still on the desk.

'Who wrote this rubbish?' demanded Granny, who had just downed her sixth tumbler of Sauterne.

'It's not rubbish, Gran,' protested Pauline. She whispered in an effort to hold Granny's voice down too.

Granny ignored the hint. She flapped the booklet in disgust. 'It's bullshit!'

'What part?' asked Minnie.

'All this stuff about why we should be proud of our district. Who wrote that crap?'

Billy was standing beside her. He hiccoughed. 'Your son wrote the whole thing. Clever, eh?'

Granny narrowed her eyes. 'Only if lying like a flounder is clever. Why'd you do it?' The booklet wagged like a reproach. 'All that stuff about the Maori wars and Te Rauparaha and Te Kooti. None of those jokers ever come within a bull's roar of this place.'

Pauline saw the look on Billy's face and snapped to his defence. 'All he's done was write down Rangi Kaawa's stories so that everybody may share them.'

Granny ignored Pauline. 'That Rangi Kaawa hasn't changed a bit. That fullah, he's so full of bullshit you's could grow roses on him!' And she laughed. She had a narrow jaw sprinkled sparingly with yellow teeth. 'Why didn't you's ask your own tupuna to tell you the true stories of the district, eh? Aue . . . I could tell plenty! Better than that rubbish.'

Billy went white. Potu grabbed his arm and glared at his mother. 'Why do you's come here and criticise, eh? Billy, he been working his butt off. What did you's do to help? If you's so full of wonderful stories, how come you's never told them to us?'

'Because you shitty-arsed little buggers never listened!' she screeched back at him.

'Please!' begged Mrs Crawford, tapping Pauline's shoulder. 'Can't you control your family? This is neither the time nor the place — '

Minnie had taken enough shit from everyone. Snatching the book from Granny she hissed at Potu: 'Cut the aggro and take Billy home, and take your mother and your useless sister too, eh. There's enough DB under the tankstand to keep them going for a coupla

122

hours.' She poked him in the small of the back. 'Hurry up, eh. Jeez — lookit how green Billy is! Silly bugger's gunna chuck up at any minute.'

She was right. Potu left grumbling about not being appreciated, but Billy just made it to the hedge by the school gate before he was noisily, messily and disgustingly sick.

Lucille glanced around. Rangi Kaawa had vanished. She peered out into the darkness and glimpsed the red rug moving across the courtyard.

Catching up to him she grabbed his arm. 'Why did you's make a fool of my father? He believed everything . . . He was so proud . . . and now he looks foolish.'

Rangi Kaawa stopped and turned, gazing down at her angry face. He understood her anger because he felt it too; in writing down those stories Billy had made fools of them all. 'I'm sorry, child. Those stories were for *mokopuna*,' he said sadly. 'They were fragile . . . like cobwebs in the wind.'

'You mean, like fairy stories?'

'Yes . . . They were never meant to be written down . . . imprisoned in a booklet.'

She watched as he shuffled away, his head bent.

Billy thought he was going to die.

'Serve you right if you do,' said Pauline. It was next morning. The kitchen was filled with the smell of bacon frying. Pauline had been up for hours. On racks on the bench half a dozen microwaved carrot cakes cooled. A big bowl of lemony icing stood beside them.

The sight and smell of all this food made Billy heave. He gulped Panadol and half-cold coffee and focused on keeping his stomach calm.

'It's going to be a lovely day,' said Pauline. 'Not a cloud in the sky.'

The youngsters came to the table. Thomas stared at his sister.

'What's those funny marks on your neck?'

Lucille kicked him. She pulled the collar of her skivvy up.

'It's a hickey, ain't it? Eeeee! I'll tell Mum.'

Pauline wasn't listening. She cracked eggs into the pan and pushed the bacon away from the spreading whites. 'One egg or two?'

'None.' Billy sat down and rested his head in his hands. He closed his eyes. The room was still rocking.

Pauline said, 'Kevin Crawford made the speech to welcome everybody. Afterwards he made a bee-line for me, and I guessed he was going to make some of his sanctimonious comments about what happened to you this evening.'

'I hope you ignored him.'

'It was too good an opportunity to miss. I sailed right into him. I told him that he should complain to the hire company that nobody was sent down to supervise the marquee. I said it was a disgrace that he hadn't organised better, and that at the very least, he, as the headmaster, should've been there to help. D'you know where he was?'

Billy didn't care.

'He was at the RSA having drinkies with the Mayor. By the way, there was a lot of comment later on about the booklet.' She shovelled the eggs and bacon out for Thomas and Lucille.

'Comments? What comments?'

'People thought it was a real scream. They were reading bits out to each other and falling about laughing.'

124

'Thanks,' mourned Billy.

'I thought that'd cheer you up.'

Trying to get sober he stood in the shade of the tankstand, clad in singlet and shorts and holding the hose over his head so that icy water ran down over his body.

When she came out to feed the chooks Lucille said, 'Don't feel bad about the stories, Dad. People really *liked* them — that's what matters, doesn't it?'

'The bastard conned me — I'll murder him,' said Billy, knowing the threat was just hot air. He was in too much awe of that shyster to ever confront him.

Granny picked her way over from next door. 'What was all that racket in the night, eh?'

'What racket?'

Granny pointed to where Lucille's chooks squawked and dived for crusts. 'All that crowing. What you's fullahs keeping roosters for, eh?'

'They catch grubs and snails, Granny!' From Lucille.

'Hmph! The starlings and thrushes do that for free, eh? Useless bloody things, roosters . . . Worse than your father were, eh Billy . . . always crowing over nothing.'

Nefta was standing by the mended fence. Her faded red tracksuit was stretched tight over her ample buttocks. Drawing deeply on a cigarette she gazed over at the large black bruise where the house used to be.

'Don't you's fullahs think it's weird that the old place burned down same day's I were asking Pauline about it?'

The icy water had done Billy a power of good. He laughed. 'The Lord moves in mysterious ways,' he said.

Minnie sat on the back steps in the morning sun and

125

brushed Lucille's hair. It was an excuse to get away from the yap-yap-yap that hadn't stopped since her mother-in-law plonked her flax kits down on the kitchen table three nights ago.

'Just as well she came, eh. I thought I were doing quite good with my life, eh, but those fullahs, all they been doing since they arrived is point out all my faults for me. Lucky me, eh?'

'I s'pose they mean well, Auntie Minnie.'

'You reckon? I think they mean trouble.' She giggled. Her huge soft stomach jiggled against Lucille's back. 'Amazing, ain'it, how peoples don't look quite so bad when they's a few hundred miles away, huh?'

'Distance lends enchantment,' sighed Lucille, who was thinking of Felipe. 'And absence makes the heart grow fonder.' She would see him today.

'Jeez, I wouldn't put it that strong. Hey, girlie, whatsamatter with your neck?'

'Um . . .'

Minnie examined the lovebites like an aborigine examining tracks in the sand. 'That weren't no hit-and-run. Someone been pretty close to you for a pretty long time, huh?'

'Aaaah . . . You're making me blush.'

'Just mind that it's only me that makes you blush, eh.' She resumed brushing. 'Y'know, I always reckon that spiders got the right idea, eh. After they done it, the sheila spider kills the bloke and eats him.'

'But that's horrible!'

'Ah, but d'you's know why she does it, eh?'

'For food for her eggs I s'pose.'

'Naaah. It's so's the bastard can't go down the pub and skite to all his mates. Cos that's what men do, eh. Every last bloody one of them.'

'What about love? Doesn't that make things different?'

'Yeah, sure. But you's gotta make sure that it ain't a flash in the pants, first, eh.'

'You mean a flash in the pan.'

'You heard me, girlie.'

Fifteen

Though the sun still slashed a yellow sword over his eyes when he took off his shades, by ten-thirty the shitty part of Billy's hangover had gone, leaving only a residue of shame. He'd looked a right berk last night — squabbling with his family then flaking out, and to top it off spewing in the bushes like a raw kid.

Billy was sitting on a chair on a decorated truck bed on the edge of the football field waiting to officially start the show. A crowd was thickening around the truck, while out in front Mrs Crawford was lining up the schoolchildren ready for the Maori haka and action songs.

The children looked so smart that Billy's heart swelled with pride. The girls were all in white, glowing like little angels, with piu piu around their waists, Maori headbands in their hair, and — this an exotic touch dreamed up by Mary Taki — floral garlands around their necks. The boys would've done Te Rauparaha's war party proud with their extravagantly whorled facial tattoos. They wore black rugby shorts under knee-length piu piu and carried flax stalk spears crested with hunks of chook feathers.

Mr Crawford strolled along the serried ranks of boys. He looked sillier than usual in a blazer, shirt and tie together with crimplene walk shorts and long socks with the feet wrinkling over the straps of Roman sandals. A biro was tucked into the top of one sock. Occasionally he took it out to add an extra flourish to a tattoo.

'You celebrated rather too well last night, I hear,' he sneered at Billy, putting him in his place.

Billy felt contempt. The headmaster might be stalking about as if he owned the show, but Billy had the mike. From now on the reins were in his hands.

Everything looked great. The Jubilee was well under way now and running on oiled wheels. Morning teas and lunches were being prepared by a team of ladies — *his* team — right now in the senior classroom. Out behind the truck Jessie Morrison was setting up her camera ready to take the group photos while Janey helped position the two flashlamp stands.

Honi Fells was in the old schoolroom taking orders for souvenir tee shirts and acting as a guide if anyone had any questions about the old photographs and articles on display, Jim Penny was organising the car parking in the old horse paddock and Awhitu Osborne and two of his grown-up sons were tuning their guitars to accompany the action songs. Yes, the district was pulling together, showing these out-of-towners what they'd missed by moving away. Community spirit, that's what.

Billy still felt idiotic about the souvenir booklet, but he understood what had happened. He'd gone to Rangi Kaawa wanting to hear stories, and stories is what he got. It wasn't Rangi's fault. Put the old guy in centre stage and he couldn't help acting, just as he was so used to using his health as a tool for getting his own way that manipulation was second nature to him now.

Billy could even appreciate the joke, for a joke is all it was. That's what he was saying to everyone who questioned the veracity of his articles.

'Go on, eh . . . This place needed a bit of livening up, so we spiced the stories a bit, eh. History's only someone's made-up view of what really happened anyway, so you's tell me, eh, what's the difference?'

Which everybody, except Kevin Crawford, accepted. The headmaster brandished his pedantic streak like a swishing cane. 'How will this look to future generations?' he asked, adopting a tone of putting Billy on the mat. 'It's downright irresponsible of you . . . People will read this and think it's the truth.'

'Well then, maybe it'll get into the history books,' grinned Billy. What the hell. It was too late to worry now.

He felt benevolent as he surveyed the crowd. Masses of his old mates were there, a couple of old girlfriends and other identities who'd long ago moved away. Billy fielded several sly digs from the ones who witnessed his brief appearance at the wine and cheese.

'What happened to you last night eh?'

'Jeez, eh, these country boys can't hold their booze.'

'That's the Billy we remember — a piss-head from way back.'

'That's right,' said Billy to everything. No worries . . . If people were going to laugh anyway, he might as well join in.

Visitors were still arriving, but time was sliding on. Billy consulted his programme again. The official welcome to the Mayor and other Te Kuiti town councillors was supposed to begin at ten-thirty, to be followed by morning tea at eleven, then from eleven-thirty to twelve-thirty the school gymnastic team would give a display, and there would be stick and poi action songs — this while the group photos were being taken. Lunch followed at one o'clock, then his Under Seven Stone Rugby team would take to the field.

Only problem: it was now ten-forty, and the kids had

been assembled now since ten-fifteen. Billy sent Tama, one of the big boys, to scout out and see if there was any sign of the Mayor's party.

By ten forty-five the children were getting restless. It wasn't right that they were expected to stand this long in the hot sun. Granny marched over with a clutch of black-shawled cronies and told him to get on with it. 'You's young ones might not care, eh, but us ancient monuments, we want our cuppa tea,' she informed him.

Tama came running back to report that the big grey council cars were parked up the road outside the marae, where, he was told, the official party were having drinks with Rangi Kaawa and the marae committee.

Hearing that, Kevin Crawford's nostrils pinched. He stalked off towards the marae. His elbows jutted like the wings of a long-legged bird.

At ten-fifty the girls were pulling bits off their floral garlands and throwing them at the boys. Mary Taki came bustling down from the senior classroom to confront Billy. 'What you's fullahs doing, eh? Morning tea is in ten minutes, eh. That Zip's screaming its head off. How come you's ain't started yet?'

Billy told her, adding carelessly, 'It's all my fault. If I'd been sober last night I would've murdered Rangi Kaawa then and there, and this wouldn't be happening now.'

'They better get their finger out, eh?' said Mary. She turned to watch a fleet of motorbikes come cruising down across the grass. 'Jeez, what are those buggers doing here?'

Everyone shrank out of the way as the huge black machines approached. Most of the riders wore black jackets with the Death Raider skull in white on the back.

Nobody wore helmets. They stopped, clustered around the truck, people hastily moving away to make room for them.

'G'day mate!' called Larry. 'Are we early?'

Billy looked blank.

'The show was 'sposed to start at ten-thirty, right?'

'That's what you said, eh, Uncle?' confirmed Rangi and Jamie. LOVE HATE and FUCK YOU ALL read their fingers, gripping the handlebars.

The rest of the gang nodded.

Bum titty fart! thought Billy in horror. He'd been so shitfaced that he'd invited the Death Raiders to the Jubilee! His balls'd be on toast as soon as Mr Crawford found out.

Furious with himself, he stammered out the reason for the delay. Then, because the crowd were muttering angrily, he pulled himself together.

The hell with it, he thought as he switched the mike on. 'Attention please, folks. We have just received word that our Mayor has decided that on a warm morning like this, thirst is more important than punctuality. Instead of arriving here at ten-thirty as he promised, he has been for the last half hour sitting comfortably in the entertainment room at the marae where he is drinking beer with Rangi Kaawa and friends. It does not matter to him that all of us are standing in the hot sun waiting. Why should he care that we — '

Mrs Crawford rushed to the truck and stared up at him. 'Mr Williams, *please*! Talk like that could sabotage the whole Jubilee, and it's so important to Mr Crawford — '

She was interrupted when Larry jumped up onto the truck bed. The mike whistled as he took it out of Billy's hand. He blew into it, to clear the feedback. 'Okay folks, who needs a mayor anyway? You all know what a mare is, don't you? It's a horse's cunt on four legs that — ' His definition was abbreviated by Billy who guessed what he was going to say next and hastily grabbed the mike.

People were hooting with laughter as Larry wrestled it back again. 'What say we start the show without them ponces?'

Fed up with delays and wanting something — anything — to happen, the audience began clapping.

'Bonza,' approved Larry. 'A haka then. Whaddaya say to one of those good old-fashioned Maooori hakas, eh?'

More clapping. A few whistles.

The Death Raiders lined up in front of the school children. Larry led them.

'KAMATE, KAMATE! WHY DO WE WAIT?
'KAMATE, KAMATE! WHY ARE YOU LATE?'

he chanted and the others echoed him, whacking their leather-clad thighs and beating their leather chests.

The children laughed and joined in, then the crowd, shouting and clapping and stamping their feet. Jessie Morrison dashed around to the front with her camera. They chanted the same words over and over. The din was so loud that Mr Crawford, who was shepherding the dignitaries out of the marae, heard it from clear up the road.

He was not amused. Ahead of the party he came puffing across the grass, elbows springing, just in time to hear Billy announce, 'We'd have a few choruses of "Why are we waiting?" in Maori too, only there's no time to tune the guitars.'

133

Enjoying themselves thoroughly now, the crowd roared in appreciation.

Mayor Dickory was a pompous twit with watery eyes and a port wine nose. He wore a King Country Old Boys football blazer, though everybody knew that he had never been selected for a regional team in his life. Over that, he was weighed down by what looked like a burglar's haul of silver plate around his neck. After the challenge and the proper haka welcome, he made a boring speech that droned on and on and on for almost three-quarters of an hour.

Selfish bastard! thought Billy, outraged. His letter setting out the morning's programme had given the Mayor a firm ten minute limit.

Curtly he thanked the mayor in a few words, praising his wit, which, Billy pointed out, was equalled only by his brevity. 'We all truly understand what a mayor is now,' he finished. People tittered.

The mayor, not known for his intelligence, looked pleased.

Mrs Crawford looked as if she was about to faint.

Pauline missed all this. She was helping set out the morning teas, putting one piece of cake, one scone, one sandwich and one pikelet onto each of a hundred paper plates. There was quite a rivalry over whose pikelets were the neatest round, whose scones had turned out lightest. Pauline was glad that she'd opted to bake carrot cakes. Nobody else had made those.

Darcy Neville's name card was still on the table.

'Sugar! Jeez, we got no sugar!' said Mary Taki, shaking the school's tupperware container. 'We were s'posed to use this, but it's empty.'

Pauline offered to fetch some from home. She hurried out to the ute and found it blocked in all around by other cars. Muttering about Jim Penny's inefficiency in traffic control, she dashed out to the road.

A sleek blue car with dark windows was slowing down to turn into the drive. There was just one man, the driver, inside. Pauline rapped on the passenger's side window. The car stopped. The window buzzed down.

'Could you please give me a lift home — ' began Pauline, then stopped, her throat too dry to continue.

The driver was Darcy Neville.

Lucille and Felipe missed all the kerfuffle with the haka too. They'd sloped off down the back of the football field to the river flat.

Lucille gazed around at the familiar trees and ferns, wanting Felipe to share her sense of wonder in the place. Sunlight filtered through the forest canopy, speckling her face. She breathed in the mossy scent of the damp ground and felt her heart lift. 'It's so . . . so *majestic*. I love it here. Don't you?'

Felipe was anxious to share something else. 'I love it anywhere.'

'Aw, fuck off. You know what I mean.'

'You know what *I* mean. He grabbed her around the bum and pulled her hard against him so's she could feel what he wanted.

She pushed him away. 'Get off, eh. You already got me in trouble at home.' She pulled down her skivvy collar. 'I been getting told off about this.'

'Why?' He bent his head and kissed the curve of neck and shoulder, his mouth damp on her warm skin.

She shivered. 'It *means* something.'

'So?' His hands were cupping her breasts now, the

135

palms polishing her nipples through her tee shirt.

'No!' She shoved at his shoulders with the heels of her hands.

'Whaddaya mean, "no"? Whaddaya mean, eh? Yesterday you's was saying that it feels good.'

'Maybe it does feel good, but it doesn't feel right.'

'What kind of shit . . . ' He grabbed at her again and she backed away, shaking her head. 'Aw, Lucille, gizza break, eh? Is it because of the gang?'

'No . . . It's me, eh. Look, maybe you'll understand, and maybe you won't. It's just not *right*. I'm too young. Miss Pring at school says it's a mistake to embark in sexual experimentation too soon, because it can cause emotional damage.'

He stared at her in disgust. 'Are you telling me that you's won't fuck because of bloody *Miss Pring*? D'you's know what the fullahs called her at school? "Instant soft-on"! I'll betcha she's never — '

'Felipe, no! It's not because of her, it's because of me. I wanted us to talk about it, so's you'd know it wasn't something wrong with you, okay? I mean, I think about you all the time, and I feel wonderful when I see you, so I guess it means I love you. So all this . . . I'm just not ready, eh.'

He took one hand and stared at her fingers. Inside he churned with a sense of sick defeat. 'Both of us aren't ready,' he acknowledged. 'I don't want to just fuck you. Hell, I *do* want to so bad that it's exploding in my head, you know? But . . . I want to give you's something . . . else. But I haven't got anything to give. Maybe one day I will . . . y'know?'

'You're very special,' she said, wonder stirring as she realised that he understood, and better yet, that he felt the same way about her.

136

'I just wish . . . Oh, shit,' he said.

'Yeah. Oh, shit, exactly,' agreed Lucille.

Their eyes met. He still looked crushed. Tentatively, she smiled.

'It would've been awesome, but what the hell,' he said.

'It will be one day, eh?'

'You bet.' He grinned.

'Race you to the school,' she said.

She let him beat her easily. By the time they reached the football field all the hurt had gone from his eyes. She hugged him, not caring who might be watching. 'I do love you, Felipe, I really do.'

'Gerroff, me mates might see.'

'What in the world do you think you're doing, *encouraging* those thugs?' demanded Mrs Crawford. The action songs were over. People drifted up to the school to have morning tea. Billy noticed that the Death Raiders were mingling with them. He wondered uneasily whether, in the bounty of his cups, he'd promised them free registration.

'I'm waiting for an explanation.' Kevin Crawford was up on the truck beside his wife, tapping one Roman sandal on the boards.

Why are all schoolteachers so predictable? wondered Billy. It was amazing, but he just didn't care at all. He could've pointed out that two of 'those thugs' were his nephews. He could've reminded him that all of 'those thugs' had already been worth their weight in gold, thanks to Mr Crawford's false economy of hiring the marquee without making sure that they knew how to erect it.

What the hell. He couldn't be bothered arguing.

He said, 'I'll put my excuses in writing. A note for the teacher. If you like, I'll even get my mother to sign it.' And he jumped off the truck.

Mrs Crawford dashed down the steps and rushed after him, 'Mr Williams! I don't think you realise how your flippant attitude is jeopardising Kevin's big opportunity.'

Billy smiled at her. She might as well have been trapped on the other side of thick, soundproof glass.

Mary Taki came hurrying to meet them. 'Oh, Mrs Crawford! Do you's have any spare sugar at home? We've run out, eh.' She turned to Billy. 'Pauline went to get some from home. She left ages ago and she hasn't come back. I do hope she's all right.'

'You look wonderful. Not a bit . . . different to what I . . . what I remembered. I've thought . . . about you so often over the years, but I never imagined . . . '

Darcy was so shy that his voice kept choking up, like an engine running on the wrong fuel.

'Me, too,' said Pauline. She felt even shyer.

But Darcy had changed. He still had that boyish lick of dark hair that flopped over his forehead, the same very white teeth and melting smile, but when he wasn't smiling his face fell into tired lines and a haunted expression seeped back into his dark eyes. Clearly, he was a man with an intimate knowledge of pain.

Pauline could see why. Under the expensive fabric of his tailored trousers one thigh looked strong and normal, while the other was so thin that the fabric fell loosely over it. Behind him, within easy reach, an aluminium crutch leaned against the back seat.

For an hour or more they had been talking and laughing, but now the mood had fallen sombre.

'I suppose I was a wimp all along,' he said. 'I should have refused to go through with that marriage. Neither of us wanted it.'

'No. You had to marry her.'

It was true. There were draconian rules in those days. If a girl got pregnant and the boy didn't want to marry her, her alternative was to answer an ad in the *Herald: Kind home offered to expectant mother in return for light household duties*. Which meant shame and slavery, and giving the baby up for adoption. Pauline knew several girls that had happened to, and she wouldn't wish it on her bitterest enemy.

'I shouldn't have stayed, though. I wasn't happy, but instead of leaving her I kept on hanging in there just hoping things would get better. And lots of times they did. Life's most treacherous trait is that it keeps changing direction. Just when you think, "Right, that's it, that's enough," something good happens, and before you know it, those long fingers of habit lie on your arm, delaying you.'

'I know.'

'Besides, you were married and out of reach.'

'I didn't waste any time going the same way, did I?' said Pauline. 'Only with me it was more a case of no longer caring what happened.'

'Is he good to you?'

'Same as everyone. Good and bad.'

'A few drinks and a careless moment. We stuffed it up, didn't we?'

'No,' said Pauline. 'We did the best we knew how.'

'That's the trouble. It had no hope of being the best. After you it was like going from sunshine into shade.'

They were sitting side by side in Darcy's car, looking through the smoked glass at the old timber mill. It was windy here at the end of the road, and desolate. From the willow trees all around the empty parking lot, pale yellow leaves swirled down. They fluttered against the windscreen. Layers of them buttered the ground.

Pauline had always thought of the deserted mill as a pretty spot. Today it looked so sad that she wanted to cry.

Darcy leaned over and kissed her. As she turned her face to meet his she shuddered inside with a slow, gentle tremble of exquisite tenderness. Her soul had not forgotten him.

Sixteen

Bobo Penny counted the last-minute registration money, locked the cash box away in Mr Crawford's desk, and went searching for Billy.

She found him watching the Under Seven Stone rugby team's demonstration of tackling, passing and goal kicking. In this chilly wind he was skimpily dressed in jeans, a peaked red cap and a red tee shirt that announced: WAIMATUA ONE HUNDRED YEARS— I RETURNED TO THE SOURCE. Pinned to his back was a sign saying: YES, I'M FOR SALE, AND BLACK, WHITE OR RED ALL OVER. SEE HONI FELLS AT THE OLD SCHOOL BUILDING TO PLACE YOUR ORDER. Bobo was too cross to ask Billy what he thought he was worth. She said, 'Did you invite the Death Raiders to the Jubilee?'

'Oh, no!'

Thomas had fumbled an easy pass.

'Billy, what *are* they doing here?'

'Leave it out, eh? Don't you get on my back too. Come on! Get stuck into it, Gary! Wake up Mark! Pick your feet up! You fullahs aren't a bunch of old ladies, you know.'

'Billy! They can't just gatecrash! Be realistic, will you, eh? Mrs Crawford's giving me arseholes and I don't blame her. Just look around you, eh. Those guys are *terrorising* people.'

That was putting it a bit strong, though Billy had to

admit he'd noticed an uneasiness on people's faces, and the way they moved away if the Death Raiders came near.

'Not a one of them has paid, you know. They're just helping themselves as if they own the place. You should have seen them hoe into lunch!'

'That's the boy, Thomas! Good stuff!'

She stood right in front of him, blocking his view. Wind whipped strands of hair around her face. She looked beautiful, her plum-coloured lips kissable in rage. 'I mean, when I asked that big fellow where his identification was, he showed me his tattooed arm, eh, and then had the nerve to boast that he had a few other bodily decorations that I would find much more interesting.'

She pretended to shudder, though Billy could tell she was taking a woman's delight in being shocked. 'Then he said he and the boys were staff and I said, "Staff?" and he said, "Come closer and I'll show you if you like." I mean to say, how *crude!*'

Billy wished he could remember what he'd said last night. Were the Death Raiders just killing a few hours or did they intend to hang around for the whole programme? Shit, he hoped not. He moved so's he could watch as Thomas made another brilliant catch, then passed the ball on in a dazzling manoeuvre. Hell, but the boy was improving... Billy could practically see the All Black jersey!

'Billy, will you *talk* to me about this?'

'Mr Williams, sir!'

Nigel Taki was shouting at him. He was needed on the field now, to help with the kicking demonstration.

Thank goodness . . . 'Gotta go. Sorry.'

'The hell you are, Billy Williams!'

142

He blew her a kiss.

She gave him the fingers.

'I kicked the ball over *six times* without missing once!' Thomas was crowing in triumph.

'That's wonderful, dear,' said Pauline.

'I done better than anybody. Even them Taki kids. I kicked higher.'

'You practise hard. You deserve to do better. I'm just sorry I didn't see it.'

'Where were you at lunchtime, Mum?'

Where was I? In heaven! In hell. . !

'Aaah, I was busy.'

Thomas scowled. 'Lucille she pinched my cake and she gave it to that stupid gang member. I wanted you to make her give it back, but then he ate it and it was too late.'

Darcy Neville was standing near the goal posts, surrounded by a flock of autograph seekers. A few of the mothers, including Bobo Penny, watched from nearby. They looked like cats watching a mouse. As Darcy handed back a signed book to the twins he raised his head and smiled in Pauline's direction.

'Mum, you're not even *listening*!'

'Mmmm,' said Pauline.

The Misses Morrison tried ringing bells, blowing whistles and sending messengers to round everybody up for the panoramic picture but by this stage people were sick of posing in their year lots and had better things to do, like laugh over the old pictures in the old school block, or better still, drift down to the macrocarpa hedge where the beer tent was set up. In the end it took Awhitu Osborne and his two lads to start singing 'Ten

Guitars' in harmony to get everyone's attention. That, and closing the bar. Everybody liked 'Ten Guitars', so it was often chosen as a signal at functions. When people heard the familiar song they soon came flocking across to the semicircular slope below the school buildings.

Here the ground had been carved out in a grassy amphitheatre with the idea of eventually installing a plastic-lined swimming pool, a scheme which never eventuated. On a sturdy tripod Jessie had set up a special Widelux camera borrowed from a friend at the Northern King Country Camera Club.

As people arrived on the slope she and Janey ranged them up the bank. On a row of chairs in front sat Mr and Mrs Crawford, past headmasters, old school staff, Darcy Neville, Mayor Dickory and the town councillors and members of the committee. Everybody else stood behind them. They linked arms, the Death Raiders right in amongst them, and sang along with Awhitu and his boys.

The mayor fawned over Darcy. It was 'Ace this,' and 'Ace that,' and 'Our boy Ace here — '

Nefta stood behind Rangi Kaawa. She had taken a shine to the old man. As she fussed, plucking red rug fibres off the shoulders of his suit, she told him he was the most distinguished man present.

When the music stopped Jessie spoke into Billy's microphone. 'What we are doing now, is making a strip photograph or a panorama. The camera will be pointed at one end of the slope.' She pointed.

'Then, over the space of five seconds it will swing slowly around to the other end of the slope.' She pointed to the other end.

'The result will be a single long photograph with

everybody in it. Because the exposure is so slow, any movement will come out as a milky blur. Please keep very, very still while the process is taking place. Remember, we have one chance and only one to do this.'

Felipe and Lucille were somewhere in the middle of the rows. He nudged her in the ribs.

'I been in one of these before, at intermediate, eh. Here, lemme show you a trick.' Towing her behind him he dodged through to the first end of the row.

'Whatsamatter with you's two?' asked Mary Taki. 'Keep still, can't you's? You's heard the lady.'

Felipe told her what he had in mind to do.

Mary grinned. She liked fun as well as the next person. As it happened, the next person heard Felipe too and passed it on, and pretty soon all of that end of the slope was buzzing like a hive on a hot afternoon. It stopped when Janey came and positioned herself in front of them for the start of the exposure.

'Are you ready?' asked Jessie over the mike. 'When I point at you, say, "Cheese!"'

'Sex!' cried everyone at that end when she pointed.

Janey's head swung around. 'This is serious!' she said.

She found herself talking to a departing swarm. As the camera lens moved along everybody from around her bolted, heads down behind the back row, unseen by the camera as they raced ahead of it, scrambling to reposition themselves on the other end. Halfway along, Felipe and Lucille stuck their heads up for a fraction of a second before moving on.

Jessie saw what was happening, but because the shutter had been tripped there was nothing she could do. Grimly she positioned herself at the far end. Janey hurried to the front and turned off the camera when the shutter clicked.

Jessie had lived in the district all her life. Everybody knew she was prim, upright and God-fearing. Even her dogs had never heard her utter the language that she spluttered into the hand-held microphone at that moment, when she realised that her one precious negative had just been wasted.

'You illegitimate . . . fornicating . . . miserable ex . . . excr . . . ' Her voice echoed around the amphitheatre. Then there was a silence of perfect completeness.

'Let's hear it for the Misses Morrison and their magic camera!' cried Billy, clapping. Everybody joined in, whistling and stamping and cheering.

And a magic camera it was. What else could record a party of 198 people when only 162 were in attendance?

Lucille and Felipe appeared three times in the photograph, giving the picture a special symmetry. The Morrison ladies were less fortunate; they seemed not to appear at all. Because she turned around in indignation at the first moment of exposure, Janey's head was depicted as the warned-of white blur, while at the opposite end Jessie wore an expression so thunderous that nobody who saw the photograph ever recognised her.

'Great show, mate,' said Larry, thumping Billy on the back.

'I would've thought this sort of thing was a bit dull for you lot,' said Billy hopefully.

'I thought so too. But it's bonza. Absofuckinlutely bonza. Thanks for the invite, mate.'

'Don't mention it.' He looked at Larry's broad, tough face, at his flax-knotted wild hair and at the greasy bulkiness of him, and shrank inside. How the hell did one go about un-inviting a motorcycle gang?

'Y'know, people usually want to keep us away from do's.'

'No kidding?'

Larry showed his large, yellow teeth. He knew sarcasm when he heard it. 'Yeah, mate. No kidding.'

'Well, did you get rid of them?'

As Larry and his henchmen drifted away, Mrs Crawford, all bluster, came stalking over.

'No, I didn't.'

'Why not? If you don't mind my saying so, just now was the perfect opportunity. I suppose you're scared of them. Is that it?'

Of course I'm fucking scared of them! But he said defensively, 'I didn't chase them off because we need them here.'

Her husband arrived in time to hear that. His nostrils pinched into a leathery beak as he said, 'We've already discussed security and I told you quite plainly — '

Rage ignited behind Billy's aching eyes. 'We need them. That marquee would still be lying in a mess of canvas on the ground, 'cept for the gang. Tomorrow the whole caboodle has to come down again, and everything has to be packed up the way it came. Gonna be a bugger of a job, I guarantee.'

'I fail to see what that has to do — '

'Tell me, do you know how to dismantle a marquee?'

'Not exactly, but — '

'I don't know either, Mr Crawford. Nor does Potu, nor does Honi, or Awhitu. While you's were knocking them back at the RSA and leaving us to it, we all tried to put it up, but we couldn't. It's one hell of a complicated thing. But Larry does know. So we need him, eh. If you's don't want him here, you tell him to go. But if he goes, I'll tell you this much, matey: you's can bring that thing down by yourself. Get that? By yourself. Me and the others, we'll be arse in the wind, down the coast — stay at my sister Nefta's place. Good whitebaiting down there at the moment.'

He turned and banged slap into Bobo. On her face dawned an expression of understanding.

She tagged after him. '*Why* didn't you tell me this before?' She squeezed his hand adoringly. 'I feel such a fool, telling you off like that. Oh, Billy, I was *awful* to you.'

'You were.'

'How on earth can I make it up to you?'

'I'll give the matter careful consideration.'

'You devil!' But she smiled. Bobo had a gorgeous smile, especially when there was a hint of promise in it.

'Minnie!' hissed Potu.

She was seated at a barbecue table under the macrocarpa trees drinking Jim Beam and Coke. There was a breeze filtering around the tree trunks; Potu disturbed her as she was cupping one hand around a ciggie in her third attempt to light it.

She gave him one glance. 'Give over, eh. Them's my lungs. You's mind your own business for a change, eh?'

'I'm not on about your smoking, eh. Come here, girlie. Come and look at this.'

'You come . . . you's should look at your stupid sister.' She gestured towards the counter, where Nefta was hunched on one of the packing crates that served as bar stools. Rangi Waaka sat on the next crate. He was talking and nodding, feigning interest.

'She's coughed up for half a dozen beers so far for that useless old shyster. Good work if you can get it, eh? I wonder how she'll get him into bed? Hide a bottle of whisky under her nightie and dare him to come look for it, I guess.'

Potu beckoned again.

Grumbling, Minnie heaved out from behind the barbecue table and followed her husband over to the horse-paddock fence.

'Look at that.'

'Look at what?' She squinted her eyes against the drifting smoke from her ciggie.

'Over there. Past the orange car. Right in the corner. Here, you's can just see them from here.'

'That couple kissing?'

'I dunno if they're kissing.'

'Might as well be, eh? Hey, that's Ace Neville, ain't it?'

'Can you's see who he's with?'

'Jeez,' wheezed Minnie. She went cold all over. 'Far out! Billy'll go spare!'

'Only if somebody tells him, eh,' warned Potu.

She could tell that he was terribly worried, but not knowing how else to react she rounded on him. 'Then mind you's keep that loose lip of yours buttoned, eh? Jeez, I don't believe what I'm seeing.'

Pauline sang as she brushed her hair, as she applied fresh makeup and dressed for the big 'do'.

Lucille drifted into her parents' room and came to a bouncing rest on the new bed. She was already groomed, her hair arranged spectacularly by Minnie into a ponytail wound through with pencil braids and gold ribbon to match her mini-dress and stockings.

'It was awesome of you to buy me this dress,' she said.

Pauline concentrated to apply her lipstick. After she blotted it and studied the effect she said, 'About time we splashed out, I'd say. We hardly ever treat ourselves, do we?'

Lucille watched the new silver and turquoise earrings being fixed into place. 'You're spending heaps lately. Did we win Lotto?'

'Aaah, wish'd be a fine thing. It's . . . it's just a small bequest.' The lie clung to her like something distasteful and she hurried to shake it off. 'But never mind that. How do I look?'

'Awesome.'

Her dress was blue and silver, with a tight bodice, cap sleeves and a swirling skirt. Just the sort of thing she used to wear years ago, when —

'Mum, how did you meet Dad?'

'Oh . . . ' Turning quickly back to the mirror Pauline half-closed her eyes and pretended to check her eyeshadow. 'We met at the pictures. A blind date . . . *Lawrence of Arabia*, I think. Yes, that was it. All that heat and sand! I've never been so thirsty. At half-time everyone in the theatre rushed out for Cokes, milkshakes, lemonades . . . In five minutes flat the Nibble Nook had run right out of drinks.'

'That's not what Dad reckons.'

'Oh?'

'Dad said he went to go home after some football do and you were in his car, crying your eyes out, eh. He said that he had only the vaguest idea who you were right then, but he drove you back home to your place, and then the next week he started taking you out. Is that true?'

'Of course it's not true!'

'Aaah . . . I thought it sounded too dumb. Mills and Boon stuff, eh. He made it up, right?'

'Right.'

She stared at herself in the mirror, remembering. Yes, Billy made up some of it. It wasn't his car. It was his father's. And it wasn't a football do, it was the annual King Country sports awards presentation dinner. Darcy had just taken her for a stroll outside. Instead of the proposal she was expecting — they'd been looking in the window of The Constantinople Jewellery Shop only the night before – he told her that Isobel Flanders, their coach's daughter, was pregnant and that his future had all been decided for him. He blurted on, some rubbish about getting drunk and being set up with her down at Feilding a couple of months before. His voice was so flat that she thought he was joking — was *sure* he was joking . . . And then he'd started to cry. She'd never heard a man cry before.

'You're not listening again!'

'Oh, sorry dear.'

'What about Auntie Minnie? How did she and Uncle Potu meet?'

'Ah . . . He was shooting rats down at the Te Kuiti dump when she went down to drop off some rubbish. She told him off and took his rifle away.'

'Get off the grass.'

'Then ask her. I don't know if she ever gave it back.'

Far out! thought Lucille in disgust. Shooting rats at the dump! A story like that was almost enough to put you off romance.

Seventeen

'Isn't this the greatest?' said Potu, trying to feel jolly as he gazed around at the crowd gathered in the marquee. Pauline was helping set out food on the smorgasbord tables but there was no sign yet of that bastard Ace Neville. Hope flickered that maybe she'd been kissing the smarmy sod goodbye. Warmed by a rush of protective brotherhood he punched Billy's arm. 'Good stuff, bro. I mean, all this, you's done great, eh.'

'Hey, that don't sound like you.'

'Nah. You's should be proud, eh. Here, lemme shout you a jug.'

Billy's eyes narrowed. 'You been on the weed?'

'Eeeh, give over. I'm serious, man. This shit about pride in our district, eh. I mean, how can you's be proud of a bunch of crap that might or might not have happened, and if it did anyway, it was so way back that who cares? This is what you's got to be proud of, eh, the here and now.'

Billy stared at his brother. Bloody hell but Potu was right! Billy had heaps to be proud of. He'd worked damned hard, far harder than other times when he'd been able to ease half the load on to Pauline. And even that booklet was a triumph—people had complimented him on the cover and laughed at his wit. He'd lost track of the number of times he'd been called a bloody brilliant comedian.

He grabbed the mike. 'Who are we?' he yelled into it.

Chatter stopped. Heads turned.

'Well? WHO ARE WE?'

'We're the Death Raiders, mate!' From Larry. He and the others occupied one of the front tables, a black mass in their own oasis of empty seats.

'Come on everybody! You know who we are! We're the WAIMATUA WALLIES AND WE WEALLY SHOULD BE PROUD!'

There were titters. Blank stares.

Billy tried again, waving a rolled up Jubilee booklet like a conductor's baton, and this time a few cautiously joined in, then again, and a few more. On the third go the crowd were on their feet, shouting along with him, 'We're the WAIMATUA WALLIES AND WE WEALLY SHOULD BE PROUD!'

Mrs Crawford forged through to the dais. She wore a dark red dress that matched the anger in her face. 'Have you gone crazy?'

'HAVE WE GONE CRAZY?'

'NO! WE'RE THE WAIMATUA WALLIES AND WE WEALLY SHOULD BE PROUD!'

At the bar, Granny nudged Nefta.

'That's my boy, eh. Got them going right off.'

'Yeah . . . Hey, they got no Drambuie, eh. D'you's reckon Mr Waaka would like a double brandy instead?'

Granny cackled. 'As long as he's not paying, Rangi Waaka would like anything. Jeez, that fullah could give Potu lessons in bludging, I reckon.'

Minnie heard her. 'Eeeeh! He done that years ago.'

Potu watched Ace Neville arrive. Between each step he paused, to hide his limp, guessed Potu. Light stroked the aluminium crutch. He couldn't hide that. Potu wondered about the ethics of grabbing it and hitting him over his bloody smug face with it. What annoyed Potu most was that apart from the limp, Ace Neville

153

looked every bit the prosperous businessman he was. Potu wondered sourly if the rumours about him being one of the new All Black selectors was true. Bloody fucking local hero; he should kill him right now.

'You look *fierce*!' Lucille came up beside him.

'Eeh, just thinking, eh.'

'Uncle Potu, how do you know when you're in love?'

The question rocked him. She looked so beautiful gazing at him with her huge dark eyes — she was as delicate as one of those teen dolls. If he could, he'd grab life by the neck and choke it to stop it from smearing dirt on her. He tried to smile. 'You's too young to think about that, eh.'

'I'm serious!'

'How can you tell if you're in love? Well, it's like this, eh. You's standing in a church, wearing this beautiful long white dress, eh, and hanging onto this bunch of white flowers, and the priest — '

'Oh, Uncle Potu!'

'Hey, listen up, eh. I seen that guy you's hanging around with, don't forget. Let me tell you, eh, you deserve better than a layabout.'

She flushed, and scuffed her shoe. 'Felipe's a nice guy. Everybody's prejudiced against him just because he can't get a job. It's not his fault.'

'It's his fault if he goes with the gang. Them gang members are bad news. Every one of them, eh.'

'Not Felipe. Truly not.' She blushed as she stammered, 'And nothing's happened . . . and nothing will. Okay?'

He placed his hand against her cheek. Knowing what her bloody stupid mother was doing made him feel all the more protective.

'Okay . . . But you's be careful, eh?'

'Okay . . . and thanks.'

Minnie was blundering between the tables, her buttocks nudging and bumping chairs as she went. She wore enough bright pink silk to make a medium-sized blimp. A matching bow sat atop her piled curls.

Larry saw her and choked in mid-swallow. 'Struth! Strawberry blancmange! A thousand kiddie desserts in one delicious dish!'

Her waist was corrugated in a perfection of billowing curves. Her breasts shuddered like feather pillows being fluffed up. Larry felt weak. 'A man could disappear in there and be lost for a week,' he whispered in a tone normally heard only in church or new-car showrooms. He hoped she would come by their table, but like a pink blimp caught in a wind sheer she veered away in the other direction, leaving him helpless.

He scrubbed at the row of stars under his eye. 'Who is she? Who's the giant economy size?'

'Her? That's my Auntie Minnie,' said Jamie Fells. He held out the hand that read: FUCKY. 'You's want me to get in another round, eh? Tide's gone out here.'

The Dreamers were twanging 'Sail Along Silvery Moon'. Lucille and Felipe were dancing, shy and close but not touching. Every time their eyes met they smiled.

Billy danced with Bobo. It was her idea. Bobo was already tipsy. She flirted with him and licked her lower lip, hinting of other ideas. Billy remembered her other ideas vividly. He tried to keep his mind on the speech that was reeling though his head.

Pauline and Darcy stood out by the flatbed truck. The music picked up their spirits and floated them round and round like toy boats. They talked and they talked and they talked. Pauline had never been so happy.

Billy had them in the palm of his hand. Not that they were a great audience either; they stirred and fidgeted and sipped their drinks when the boring farts of ex-headmasters rambled on about what successful headmasters they'd been. But whenever Billy grabbed that mike the place fell silent, waiting for the moment to erupt into appreciative laughter. He was even funnier than the ventriloquist act had been.

'RIGHT ON, BILLY!'

'THAT'S TELLING US LIKE IT IS!'

This time Billy held up a copy of the souvenir booklet. 'This here's a history book. It's as true as most and truer than some you's seen.'

Laughter.

'History's bullshit, right?'

'RIGHT!'

'You want some more history, eh?'

'RIGHT ON, BILLY!'

'Okay, okay. As you's know, and if you didn't know by tonight's performance you could guess. I'm a mongrel, folks. Half haka and half Highland fling. My great-grandad decided that he was too great a grandfather to spend his life hunting wild haggis in the Highlands, and besides, all them Arctic gales were blowing up under his tartan skirt and freezing his sporran to a funny shade of blue — '

He stopped, intercepting wild signals from Kevin Crawford. 'Excuse me, folks, it seems that our esteemed headmaster would like a word. No? Well my great-grandfather, being totally pissed off with this terminal

156

case of blue-sporran the weather was giving him, hopped onto a sailing ship, eh, and sailed over to Aotearoa. Well, this is where the story gets sticky, eh. Instead of doing a bit of peaceful settling as he had in mind, he fell straight into the hands of a tribe of wild Maori.'

'Worse than haggis any day!' interjected Awhitu Osborne.

'Right! He was terrified! He thought he'd fall straight into their hangi next, but luck was on his side. One of the Maori maidens rescued him, eh. But she had plans of her own.' He grinned delightedly at the audience. 'Evil plans! She took him captive, held him in her hut for weeks and forced him to do all sorts of things to her . . .'

'TELL US WHAT THINGS, BILLY!'

'Aaah . . .'

'GO ON, BILLY!'

'Nah. All the kids amongst you's know what I'm referring to, but there's some old folks here, and they might be shocked if I go into details . . .'

Everybody roared with laughter.

'They might not even BELIEVE me . . .'

Mrs Crawford looked furious.

'And schoolteachers,' added Billy wickedly. 'They'd be even more shocked, eh. Schoolteachers don't even know about things like that. Do you know how schoolteachers make little schoolteachers? Shall I let you in on the secret? They don't compound sins, folks. They compound fractions. Vulgar fractions.'

It wasn't that funny, but the place broke up.

'Jeez Billy, you's crazy or what?' said Mary Taki. 'Them schoolteachers will lynch you's, eh.'

From Granny: 'Good on you son. Betcha everybody here would like to cheek their teacher the way you cheeked that up-himself sod Mr Crawford. I never seen a man as mingy as that one, eh.'

'Pauline will be overjoyed, at least. You'll never be asked to be on a committee again,' remarked Bobo.

'Where is Pauline, anyway?' said Nefta.

'She's around,' said Minnie quickly. 'I seen her just a minute ago.'

At supper Felipe piled his plate high. Lucille took just one drumstick and nibbled on that.

Opposite, her mother leaned against one of the supporting poles. She had a dreamy look on her face that Lucille had never seen before. Lucille thought that she looked as beautiful as a movie star.

Suddenly she smiled. It was more like a beam of soft light radiating out of her face. Lucille turned her head to see who she was smiling at.

At the table behind her sat Ace Neville. As Lucille watched he put his fingers to his lips and blew her mother a kiss. Lucille felt unreal. Far out! Her mother and Ace Neville! She shook her head. That kiss must have been meant for someone else. She must have been mistaken.

Bobo had never been so turned on. It wasn't just the booze, or that twangy Hawaiian music that always did twisty things to her insides. It was more than that; the way the crowd reacted to Billy made her feel wild all over. He was the local hero now, even more than Ace Neville, who, let's face it, was a wrecked has-been anyway. A real disappointment. When she asked him to have a waltz with her he said he couldn't dance and didn't even offer to buy her a drink.

But now she'd lured Billy up to the old classroom. It was pitch dark and deserted, full of the smells of smoke and flower arrangements.

That twangy music was still going; it made Bobo feel as if she itched everywhere at once, in a frantic and delicious way.

'Let's fuck,' she whispered.

He hadn't heard her say that for years. As he reached for her, excitement crammed his head so hard that even his eyes felt tight in their sockets. He smothered her mouth with his, fumbling under her skirt with one hand as he groped for his zipper with the other.

'Let me do that.'

'Hey,' he said as his hands slid over smooth warm skin. 'Where's your knickers?'

'Where do you think?'

He grabbed at his discarded jacket, fumbled and pulled out something soft and satiny.

'You devil!' It was an old trick of hers during their affair that at PTA meetings or at picnics or dances — once even at church — she would bump up against him and slip her panties into his pocket. It drove him crazy.

'When did you put them there?'

'When we were dancing.'

His scalp went cold. That was before the speeches. At any time during the evening he could've groped for a handkerchief and in front of all those people pulled out Bobo Penny's knickers!

She laughed wickedly. 'I kept hoping you'd find them.' Before he could say anything she slid her tongue into his mouth and flicked it all around the inside of his lips, arousing him to an even more frantic pitch of desire.

He groaned as his hands slid over her smooth buttocks and slid through her damp bush, his fingertips finding the firm, moist bud. When she eased his trousers over his hips and his cock sprang free, he thought it would burst. In a panic of excitement he slammed straight into her.

She arched back with a groan, then clung to him, clenching her legs around his back, sobbing for breath as she thrust her hips against him.

'Billy, do you love me?' she gasped as she came.

Bursting with self, driven by self, Billy pounded into her again and again. He didn't even hear her.

At that moment, Darcy and Pauline were lying in each other's arms on a rug spread under the trees at the old mill. The blue dress was bunched around Pauline's waist, flattened by Darcy's weight as he lay between her legs. They were kissing and making love at the same time, very slowly and tenderly.

Every few seconds Darcy would stop and lift his head, smiling down into her eyes. 'You're so beautiful . . . I can't believe this is happening.'

She lifted the strand of hair off his forehead. 'Nor can I. After all these years. It's incredible to think that this is our very first time.'

Pauline's whole body strummed with a sharp-edged joy. She felt she was dreaming, hallucinating. Every time Darcy moved even slightly ripples radiated through her as if from pebbles dropped into a pond. She felt wonderfully happy, yet sad at the same time. It was as though the lulled part of her mind knew that this was only a dream from which she soon would wake.

After he took her home, Pauline stood on the front

lawn in the dark. Through the lighted kitchen windows she could see Billy making himself a cup of Milo.

Not wanting her dream to end she had to force herself to walk up the steps and open the back door. Billy looked up when she came in. Though it was past two he didn't ask where she'd been, just if she wanted some Milo too.

'Don't you care why I'm late home?'

He was surprised in a blurred-around-the-edges kind of way.

'Should I?'

'I suppose not.'

As he gulped his Milo, some splashed down the front of his shirt. He wasn't drunk, just so high that he was still up there on top of the world, but at the same time more tired than he'd ever been in his life. Everything had gone so well.

'Except for Lucille,' he said. 'She should've won that essay competition. Got her head full of that boy, that's the trouble. Gotta do something about that. Nip it in the bud.'

'Aaah, she's all right.' Pauline sat opposite and stirred her Milo. 'You putting the hangi down in the morning?'

'First thing.'

He'd been drunk so often lately that it seemed strange to be talking to him in the kitchen in the middle of the night. 'Three dozen frozen chickens arrived just as we left tonight. Don't forget to take them . . . They're thawing out under the tankstand.' He yawned and nodded at the same time.

After checking Lucille and Thomas, Pauline sat alone in the kitchen sipping her Milo and making it last a long time. The dreamy, tender feeling came back; she pulled it around her like a rug and hunched inside it, thinking with wonder about what had happened tonight. She waited until she heard Billy's snoring before she went into the bedroom. Then she lay awake for a long time, smiling into the darkness.

Eighteen

'KAKAKAKA KAWWW!'

Billy groaned. It was three-thirty, and he was knackered.

'KAKAKAKA KAWW!'

Four-fifteen, awake again. He thirsted for sleep.

At five o'clock he put the pillow over his head.

'KAKAKAKA KAWW!'

Bloody rooster. If he wasn't too tired to move he'd go out there right now and throttle the bastard.

Then, suddenly, it was daylight. He looked at the clock. Eight o'clock! Hell — he was supposed to be down at the school helping with the hangi. He staggered out, clutching the door jamb for support.

'Morning!' said Lucille, looking radiant. The sight of her jolted him awake. He wanted to have a couple of words with her about that kid she was mooning over last night: words like NO WAY! He followed her into the kitchen.

As she set out the plates she was singing. Bacon hissed in a pan, toast flopped from the toaster. 'What would you like, Dad? Just say the word and I'll fix it, eh?'

Unable to bring himself to dash that happiness from her eyes, he shambled off to the bathroom and poked a razor around his face. Hell, a fucking *gang member*: he couldn't let that go by, he had to say *something*. Unless . . . maybe he could shove it on to Pauline. Aaah . . . smart move; besides, she'd be able to lay down the law without coming over too heavy.

As he was backing out of the drive he remembered the three dozen frozen chickens. By now they were well thawed. He'd slung the damp cartons into the back of the ute when Lucille came out with her basin of bread scraps for her chooks. Suddenly he had a brainwave.

'That rooster of yours has woken me once too often. You better stay inside, eh. You's don't want to see this,' and lifted his branch-trimming axe from its bracket behind the cab.

Lucille was horrified. Pleading, she followed as her father marched around to the back of the house.

Grumpy, Doc and Dopey came dashing as soon as they saw her. They squawked with excitement, extending their necks as they ran; too late Lucille realised that just by being there she had unwittingly made it all too easy for her father.

He was so quick. Moving in a blur he grabbed Doc and clamped him under one arm. Lucille could do nothing to stop him.

'Please, Daddy, please!'

'Don't watch,' he warned, as he went behind the woodshed.

There was a thunk.

Lucille screamed.

He emerged with the axe. She didn't see him because her hands were over her eyes.

'A good job well done,' he said. 'Here, you'd better deal with this,' and he handed her something heavy and wet.

She screamed again, then saw that it was a thawed, oven-ready chicken in its plastic wrapping.

'What? Where's Doc?'

As she spoke her pet came whirring around to greet her. He looked indignant and ruffled, but unharmed.

164

'You didn't kill him?'

'Course I didn't kill him. He's your pet, isn't he?'

'Oh, Dad!' She wanted to hit him. She wanted to hug him. She wanted to cry.

'We'll have to make a proper house for your chooks. One with the perch up close to the roof. If they can't stretch upwards they won't crow. I'll fix it later. I promise.'

'You promise.'

They grinned at each other. Billy felt suddenly awkward. 'I only want what's best for you, you know that, eh.'

'I know, Dad.'

'This gang thing. It worries me, eh. You's my little girl and I trust you, but this gang thing I don't like to see. You understand, eh?'

She hung her head, nodding.

He tipped her chin up and kissed her on the nose. 'Okay . . . Take care, girlie.'

'Thanks, Dad.'

Potu opened the Sunday papers. 'Hey . . . It's no-smoking day.'

Nefta, Gran and Minnie sat at the other three sides of the table. All were drawing hard on ciggies. All had cynical eyes slitted against the smoke. The communal ashtray was heaped to overflowing.

'You're full of shit,' said Nefta.

'Same old shit at that,' said Minnie.

'No way.' He showed them the headline: WORLD DECLARES A SMOKE-FREE DAY. 'See?' he said.

They refused to take him seriously.

'Hey, maybe that means that ciggies are going for free today, eh,' said Nefta.

'That'd be great!'

'It means you's supposed to exercise some self-control,' said Potu. 'Lay off the fags for just one day, eh? See how much better you'd be for it.'

'Why don't you's lay off the nagging?'

'You's sound like a broken record.'

'Yeah, nag — nag — nag. You's worse than an old woman — and I should know, eh.' And that from his own mother.

'Listen, you's! It's only one day! Give it a go, at least, eh?'

They laughed until Potu gave up and left in disgust. There was no respect for a man in a house full of women.

He'd meant to stop by Billy's place and see if he could have a word with Pauline — just a friendly warning hint to keep away from that slimeball Ace Neville — but he was so angry with his womenfolk that he forgot until he was almost at the school. Then he thought about Billy and Bobo. There was something queer in the way she was looking at him last night, like she was looking for a good feed and he was on the menu.

Ah, shit, he thought. Who was he to point the finger at anybody? Best let the whole thing drop.

'Dad's a rascal!' said Lucille.

Down at the school she was recounting the incident of Doc and the axe to Pauline and the other women who were helping make the tea. Dozens of cups and saucers were set up on paper-covered trestle tables outside.

The ladies were in fits. All but Pauline. She didn't even smile, just acted as if she had a lot on her mind.

'He said he'd build me a chook house for them. He promised!'

Pauline had to laugh at that. 'Well . . . if he promised, it'll happen then, won't it?'

By the time the soil was shovelled off the hangi mound and the layers of steaming sacking pulled back, most of the other work had been done.

The marquee was down and packed. With Larry organising it had taken less than half an hour. Some of the out-of-towners helped. Felipe had been assisted in his task of bundling up the ring poles by Gordon Pryce, an old boy from Hawke's Bay. Pryce, a farmer, was impressed by the way Felipe took Larry's instructions to the letter, and how strong and willing he was.

'How long you been in the gang, boy?' he asked.

Felipe hung his head. 'Not in it yet, eh,' he mumbled. 'Maybe I'll get patched next year. If I'm lucky, eh.'

'You could get even luckier,' mused Gordon.

Afterwards the farmer noticed that instead of standing around cracking tinnies with the others, Felipe went off to help the women restore the classrooms to order. He did that without being asked.

'Good lad, that,' he decided, and went to talk to him.

Now everybody queued for food. After lunch people would drift away; some had a long way to travel.

The food smelled wonderful: pork and lamb and pumpkin, cabbage, kumara and potatoes. There was even eel from the river and wire-netting baskets of mussels and pipi that had been steam-cooked with a compressor.

The food was served in true Maori fashion, in plate-sized flax baskets that the schoolchildren had made in history studies. Mrs Fells, Mrs Osborne and Titewhai

Kaawa dished generous helpings as the guests filed past with their baskets. Lucille and Felipe sat under the trees in the shade to eat theirs. She brushed a wasp away from her meal, as Felipe told her about his job offer.

'I'm going to do fencing, and learn shearing. Mr Pryce said that maybe I can even drive the tractor. Neat, eh.'

Lucille said nothing.

'Hey, eat up. I thought you liked hangi food. No good when it's cold, eh.'

'I guess with what you told me, I got no appetite.'

'But it's great news.'

'I know . . . oh, I know that.'

'I been feeling so useless for so long, and then out of the blue — here comes a job offer. Bloody fantastic, I reckon.'

'It's fantastic. I agree, and I'm happy for you . . . but you's going away, and I won't see you again.'

'Hey, Hawke's Bay ain't far. I'll come home for holidays.'

'But that won't be for ages.'

'Aaah, no worries, eh. You'll be older then, and . . . '

He whispered in her ear.

She pushed him away. 'Ah, fuck off!'

'Maybe, eh?'

She was blushing. 'Maybe.'

The hangi was as much of a success as the evening before had been. Awhitu Osborne and his two grown-up sons played and sang country and western tunes with Maori lyrics. Some of the school children clustered around to sing along too. Their cheeks and chins were polished with grease from the food.

Disdaining the flax baskets Janey and Jessie Morrison brought their own china plates, knives, forks and picnic set from home. Jessie had planned a candid feature of photographs of the hangi to submit to the *King Country Gazette*, but she was so narked about yesterday's panorama fiasco that she changed her mind.

'Let them stew in their own juice!' she declared obscurely.

Rangi Kaawa sat in regal splendour on a chair Nefta carried all the way down from Mr Crawford's study. She queued for his helping and broke his food up into small pieces before handing him the basket.

'Eeeeh,' he sighed in satisfaction as she spread a paper napkin in his lap. He adored being fussed over. To Granny he said, 'Your mokopuna, she's a good girl, eh?'

'My mokopuna is a fool,' retorted Granny.

When the schoolchildren massed under the kowhai trees to sing 'Now is the Hour' in English and Maori, many of the visitors wept.

Pauline wept too.

'Whatsamatter, Mum?' hissed Thomas, squeezing her arm.

'Oh . . . nothing. This song always makes me cry.'

'I'll sing "The Laughing Policeman", eh? That'll cheer you up.'

'I'll be okay in a minute.' She was aware that Darcy was watching, that Darcy was leaving, and she felt as if iron gates were closing around her. They'd been there all the time, but up until now she could pretend they weren't real. Now her pretending days were over, and that frightened her.

Billy felt marvellous. He couldn't have asked for a better show. The weather really turned it on, the district pulled together and the visitors all had a great time.

Everybody sought him out to thank him.

'Fan-bloody-tastic.'

'You were a winner, Billy.'

'Awesome show. Just awesome.'

'Never forget it mate. Best reunion I ever been to.'

Billy glowed with pride. 'Nah, no big deal,' he said.

Bobo approached and pretending to tell him something, bumped against his hip. As she sauntered away, she glanced back and pursed her lips. He grinned and thrust a hand into his pocket.

His fingers encountered silky black lace.

'I love you Pauline,' said Darcy. 'I've always loved you.'

'I know.' For it was true. 'I love you, too.' That was true as well.

They were standing in a grove of totara trees watching cars lurch up the slope out of the old horse paddock. It was really over now. Pauline thrust her hands up inside the sleeves of her coat. She had never felt so cold — as if she'd swallowed a whole packet of frozen peas.

'I want you to come to the city and live with me — '

'No,' said Pauline.

'No?' Stricken, he wavered and almost lost his footing, his crutch scrabbling for purchase on the stony ground.

'I mean, I can't just say "yes" just like that. Maybe I won't ever be able to. There's lots to think about. This isn't just you and me, Darcy.' She could hardly get the words out. When she was near him she wanted to forget everything else, even the kids. Guilt prickled at her.

'There's nothing we can't resolve,' he said gently.

She nodded, feeling bleak.

'Will you call me?'

'I promise.' The words stuck in her throat.

'Will you come and visit?'

'I don't know. Maybe . . . I just don't know.'

It was no answer at all, but it would have to do.

Crying with great gulping sobs, Pauline filled the bath and climbed into it. She wanted to stop, she tried to stop, but it was like being in a car careering out of control. An awful grey, cold sorrow was wrapping itself around her so's she couldn't move, couldn't see.

The back door slammed, jolting her. Groping for a towel she wiped her face, listening. In a few seconds Lucille's door opened and shut. Through the wall she heard unmistakable sounds of her daughter's voice. Lucille was crying too.

She rapped on the wall.

Silence. Than a single, frightened, 'Mum?'

'Come in here, pet. It's okay.'

Lucille stood in the doorway. Her face was a swollen mess.

'What's the matter? Has Dad been mean again?'

'It's just a crying day, that's all. Sunday, Monday, Tearday. Hop in with me, pet. Let's have a sobfest.'

Lucille giggled and wailed at the same time. As she tugged off her clothes she spat out scraps of grief. Life was shit. It wasn't worth living. She hated school, she hated everything.

'I hear you, but what's really happened?' asked Pauline, making room for her daughter to get in.

The water rose a few centimetres as Lucille subsided and leaned her slender coffee-coloured body against her mother's plump whiteness. Pauline began to soap her back, thinking about all the years she had done this.

Then out it came. 'Felipe's leaving the gang!'

Pauline snorted; she couldn't help it.

'It's not funny, Mum. He's got a job and moving to Hawke's Bay, and he's beside himself with joy, and I feel left behind.'

'That's a sad feeling. Well worth a few tears.'

'You understand?'

'About being left behind? Ooooh, yes.'

'You're great, you know? Felipe challenged me to tell him one truly good, honest person I know, and I told him it was you.'

'That's quite a compliment, pet, but I haven't taught you very well, have I?'

'What do you mean?'

She splashed water over Lucille's shoulders to rinse off the suds. 'If nobody's completely good, then I can't be, can I?'

'Aaah, Mum. You're so near enough that it doesn't matter.' She giggled now, the tears all gone. 'Hey, I know it's not even night-time, but let's get out and get into our PJs and eat ice cream and watch *Dynasty*. There's a special re-run of our favourite episodes at six o'clock.'

Pauline sighed. *Oh, to have an elastic heart*, she thought.

Nineteen

It was drinks all round at the pub.

A reward for the helpers, as Billy explained to Michael O'Reay. He was more than happy to open up the private bar especially and to keep right on setting up the jugs and shorts and celebratory shots of crème de menthe while he totted up the prices on a running tab.

The place was crowded: Honi and Awhitu with his boys, the Takis and the Pennys and Rangi Kaawa and Titewhai — everybody who still had a spark of life in the engine after the show was over and guests departed.

Even the Crawfords were there, Mrs Crawford boring Pauline to tears. Billy had never seen her looking so glum.

'Who's paying for all this?'

Billy sighed as he set another schooner down in front of the headmaster. Trust Kevin Crawford to nitpick.

'It's like this, okay? The Jubilee never set out to make a profit, right? Well, we have. A damned good profit, too. The books are square, eh, there's a few hundred in the bank, so all we're doing is sopping up the leftovers.'

'Leftovers?'

'The late-registration money. Bobo's gone to get it now, eh. There's not much, but she reckoned there was plenty for a few rounds.'

'I see. And by whose authority are you spending it?'

'By the committee's, if you like. Drink up, Mr Crawford.'

'And who's paying for the free-loaders?' He pointed

at Granny and Nefta who were supping up as large as the rest.

'Aah, I'm kicking in for them.'

'Mind that you do!'

For a moment Billy knew exactly how murderers feel in the instant before they commit their crimes. He said, 'Jubilee went off well . . . Great show, wasn't it?'

Kevin Crawford sniffed.

'Everyone had a marvellous time, don't you think? A success all round, wouldn't you say?'

Go on, say it! But Kevin Crawford wasn't giving an inch. He exhaled slowly.

'If you must know, I was disappointed. There was no dignity. No sense of occasion. In fact, Mr Williams, since you asked me — Aaaah! You clumsy idiot!'

They both stared at the headmaster's beer-sodden lap.

'Hell, I'm sorry,' said Billy. 'Someone must've bumped me.'

'There's nobody near you!'

'Oh, you're right!' He managed to look surprised. 'Clumsy me! How in the hell did that happen?'

Michael O'Reay was there with a cloth. 'Lord be praised that it's only beer you're splashing about! That crème de menthe is *purgatory* to be liftin' out of the carpet.'

The Death Raiders had no intention of going into the pub. Larry's plan had been to strike out for Hamilton, lair up there for a bit, pull some birds, find the local skinheads and kick some ass, then drift back to Te Kuiti in a week or so.

But when they roared up the road Larry saw Minnie in the car-park. She was leaning into the window of a green Falcon ute, talking to someone in the passenger seat.

As they pulled level the ute rolled forward and Minnie waved her friends goodbye.

She turned and waddled back towards the pub entrance. She was wearing a bright yellow tracksuit. In the dusk her rump looked like two enormous suns chafing together, radiating warmth.

'Struth!' said Larry reverently.

He wheeled about, narrowly missing being run down by a long-haul bacon truck. The blare of horn nearly blasted the others off the road.

'Bottle time, boys!' Larry bellowed, and trundled back. Brushing aside his henchmen's protests, he sauntered inside. Gatecrashing was second nature to the gang, who quickly made themselves at home in the crowded room, taking over the corner table from where Larry had a good view of Minnie. Pulling birds was second nature to Larry too, but when it came to approaching a woman he truly desired, he was paralysed by bashfulness.

And Minnie was supremely desirable.

From the table below the stag's head he watched her sipping her crème de menthe. He admired the way her shoulders wobbled when she laughed. He loved the high pitch of her voice.

'Aaaah,' he sighed, his gaze lustfully fixed on her enormous bosoms. Gripping her in the throes of shuddering passion would be like pummelling an enormous squeaky toy.

His mouth watered in contemplation.

Bobo arrived back at the pub just after the Death Raiders had forged their way into the private bar and set up camp. Bobo was gasping. She tugged at Billy's arm.

'Not here,' warned Billy, glancing in Pauline's direction. Bobo's knickers were still burning a hole in his pocket.

'Not *that*, you fool. We must talk. Something terrible . . .'

He could see that something dire was wrong. Her face was flushed from running, but the skin was pinched dead white around her plum-coloured lips, as if she was having a heart attack. He glanced over to where Jim Penny was deep in conversation with a farmer from down the valley. Nothing seemed amiss there.

'Come *on!*' urged Bobo.

Apprehensive, he followed her into the corridor.

'The money! It's gone! It's been stolen!' Fright came gushing out of her like beer from a shook-up can. 'I put the cash in the tin, and locked it in the drawer. When I went back for it, the drawer had been forced open and the tin was gone. Oh, Billy! There was over four hundred dollars in there.'

Billy frowned.

Her voice was high and trembly. 'Say something! Please don't look at me like that!'

'I'm thinking.'

'I feel just terrible. But I did lock it away. It's really not my fault, Billy . . . Someone must have seen me put it in there. But who — '

There was a silence, and then she added in quite a different tone, cold and hard. 'It was those bloody gang members that you encouraged to hang around. They're not fools. They saw money change hands . . . '

'No. *No!* Don't even think like that.'

But he was already thinking it. On the one hand it was hard to credit that anybody would rip them off and then brazenly come and join in the booze-up, but the gang had their own rules. They'd never think twice about abusing hospitality.

'Billy, it must be them! They saw the money. They could easily have seen me when I walked across the courtyard with the cash box, and they were still at the school, skiving around on their bikes when I went home to freshen up. It has to be them.'

Billy patted her arm. He took a deep breath. 'Don't worry about a thing.'

She was worried before, now she was terrified. Billy looked shit-scared. As if a great big boulder was about to drop on him from a great height. The last time she had seen that expression was when Jim walked in on them four years ago.

Sensing that she was being watched, Minnie glanced over. Larry smiled at her, showing his big, yellow teeth. Minnie was puzzled. Were the gang laughing at her?

The Death Raiders were puzzled too. Jamie said, 'Hey, boss, I thought weez gonna split?'

'Yeah,' said Rangi. 'What say they find out — '

'Shuddup, willya? No worries. Relax.'

'But boss — '

Brushing off the hand that read: OUALL, Larry eased out of his chair and strolled to the jukebox, rammed in two fifty-cent pieces and punched out 'Black Magic Woman' and a couple of other numbers.

'Dance,' he said to Minnie.

'*Me?*'

'You.'

'You's crazy or something?'

'Maybe . . . ' Larry looked right into her eyes. 'You game to find out *how* crazy?'

She giggled. Quickly he grabbed, scooping an arm around her before the wobbling stopped, then closed his eyes in pure bliss. Hugging her was like falling into a cloud. He sank in at least ten centimetres all over. Black Magic Woman was right. She was bloody marvellous!

Right then Billy walked back into the bar. He had very little courage to begin with and that was right now draining away, but before the last of it swirled down the plughole he marched up to Larry. He heard the weak quaver in his voice as he said, 'Where's our money, mate?' and *that* made him really angry.

He was furious with himself. The worst part of this fiasco was that he, Billy Williams, had actually looked up to these guys. Admired them. Envied them even. Sure they were big and brash and brawly, but they were mates, right?

Wrong. That's the bit that sickened like something rotten in his gut. All the time he thought they were great guys they were really small and sneaky and thieving. Everybody had warned him about the gang, and he wouldn't listen. That pissed him off most of all.

Larry's face was smothered in Minnie's neck. She was still giggling. Even if his ears hadn't been buried in her flesh her shrieks would have made it impossible to hear.

Potu heard though, looked up, then got up. Incredible though it might seem, that bastard was messing with his Minnie. And, even more incredible, *she* was lapping it up. Choking on a mouthful of DB he spluttered, 'Hoi! Whaddaya think you's doing mate?'

Larry groaned in ecstasy and rocked his hips in the age-old message as 'Born to be Wild' belted from the juke box. He didn't see Potu, Awhitu and Honi joining Billy on the tiny dance floor.

Stoked with numb bravado, Billy whacked Larry on the shoulder. 'Where's our money?' he shouted.

Potu whacked Larry on the other shoulder. 'Leave off of my woman, *mate*!'

The Death Raiders saw the threat against their leader and leapt to their feet.

It was all on.

The women screamed and scrambled for cover. The men waded in slinging punches. Potu hammered away at Larry's face with no result until he landed a lucky blow to his Adam's apple. Honi dived into the melee and cracked Jamie and Rangi a few well-deserved whacks around the ears. Unable to retaliate by beating up their old man they cowered, holding LOVE HATE and FUCKY OUALL over their faces. Jim Penny, who was a mean fighter, bashed his way into the thick of it and in the confusion managed to stamp two satisfying fist-prints on to Billy's nose and chin before he resumed whacking and head-butting gang members.

Jugs and glasses ricocheted around the room. Beer and spirits flung out of them like banners. Crème de menthe splattered on the walls.

As Michael O'Reay saw all his hard work unravelling before his eyes he uttered a keening wail, then scampered around, nimbly dodging missiles and fists as he whisked glasses and beer jugs out of danger.

The Death Raiders fought hard but were outnumbered. In less than a minute Larry whistled, a single sharp blast between his teeth, to signal the end of the skirmish. Shouting obscenities the gang departed, leaving the Waimatua School Committee standing in the midst of the wreckage.

There was a silence that lasted until the throbbing of Harley Davidson engines had faded away.

Tenderly, Billy fingered his jaw. There was something familiar about the way one fist had cracked into him like a sledgehammer. Though sore, he felt bloody marvellous.

'We beat them! We beat the shit out of those bastards!'

'Congratulations, boys,' Michael O'Reay said, 'But we are left with one teeny tiny problem, I'm thinking. Ladies and gentlemen, who's about to be paying for all this, then?'

The money! Bobo looked at Billy. Mr Crawford looked at Billy. Michael O'Reay looked at Billy.

Billy drew Pauline aside urgently.

He whispered in her ear, explaining about the money being stolen.

'That's not *our* problem, Billy,' she hissed.

'It is and it isn't. Look . . . I started the fight, okay? Our money's sitting there. You're not using it, are you? Can't I just borrow it? I'll pay it back later. I promise.'

Wanting to refuse, she considered. The money was hers. Billy'd had his cut. As for the rest of the school committee — they could get stuffed and roasted before she'd give them a cent. She looked at his pleading, little-boy face and realised that he wasn't just asking for money, he was asking her to save him. The Jubilee had been his triumph. An ugly squabble with Michael O'Reay would sour everything.

Billy was the hero of the moment; grudgingly she decided to let him be a hero to the end.

'You don't deserve it,' she said.

'You beauty!' he said, and hugged her. She pushed him away.

Minnie was still giggling as she drove Pauline home to get the cash.

'Well, that sure was exciting, eh?'

Pauline was silent. At the moment she was bone-weary and plain disgusted with Billy. If he'd taken care of the money instead of being hell-bent on swilling at the pub, this never would have happened. And what was he doing, brawling with the gang? Didn't he have any sense at all? Only eleven hundred dollars remained in the hoard. The thought of giving up any of it made her feel ill.

Minnie changed gears with a generous crunch. 'That could've been fun, eh, 'cept for those bastards wrecking everything. Silly pricks.'

'The gang?'

'Naah. Potu and Billy. Stupid buggers. I reckon that Death Raider guy was after me. He was feeling me up, eh, like there was no tomorrow. Bet he's a good fuck, too, and those bloody men ruined it.'

That shocked Pauline out of her gloom. 'Minnie, I don't believe what you're saying.'

'You's want me to say it again?'

'Are you saying that you would've gone with that gang leader?'

'Why not? How many chances d'you's think I get?' She sliced Pauline a shrewd glance. 'Aaah, don't act like you's welded into one of them charity belts.'

Pauline swallowed; her throat was dry and she felt giddy, as if she'd suddenly been tipped upside down. Minnie's voice was so sly that she must know something. What had she guessed?

The car lurched up over the verge and rocked to a stop in the driveway. Thomas and Lucille came to peer out of the lighted lounge windows. Minnie turned to face her sister-in-law. 'I got this one rule about life, eh. I reckon that you's should do what you's want, only just make sure that the priest don't have to lie at your funeral.'

'I'm not sure I understand.'

'Just don't confess, eh. Don't you's confess nothing to nobody.'

Dazed, Pauline walked inside. The kitchen was bright and pretty, welcoming her. It was still so new that it gave her a fresh start of pleasure each time she entered. *I created this,* she thought. *This house looks lovely now, and all because of me.*

Thomas and Lucille were watching telly. Thomas had showered and changed. He smelled warm when she hugged him, but being Thomas, he wriggled free.

'Thomas!' reproached Lucille.

'Aaah shuddup!' said Thomas.

Alone in her bedroom Pauline took the shoebox down from the wardrobe shelf and impulsively took out all the money. Billy was welcome to it. He'd find a way of getting it sooner or later anyway. She might as well chuck it all in his face right now.

At the door, she turned back. Billy only needed five hundred; that other six hundred might come in handy one day. She'd bank it in her name, as her secret.

'You never know,' she said, applying fresh lipstick at her new walnut-framed mirror.

'You never know what?' said Lucille from the doorway.

'You never know your luck in the big city, of course.'

'Are you going to the city?'

Pauline watched herself blot her lips. She couldn't believe that only a few weeks ago she'd gazed at the drab woman in there and thought, Face it girl: you're a loser. Now she saw a woman who was bright-eyed and even pretty, someone who was a little stronger, wiser and happier than she had been before. Someone who felt good about being Pauline Williams.

'Are you going to the city, Mum?'

Pauline smiled at her reflection. Why not? she thought. She had been travelling along this road for so long that the scenery in her life was all too familiar. There was a lot of world out there that she had never seen. Some of it was sure to be worth a look.

'I think I might . . . one day,' she said.

So it had all turned out well in the end, thought Billy a little boozily as he and Potu made their wavery way out into the night. They'd all pitched in to clean up the mess, then had another round of drinks, and another.

The sky was ablaze, like a brightly lit city. Billy thought that he had never seen it look so beautiful. He and Potu stood unsteadily in the courtyard and unzipped their flies. It was a relaxing, companionable moment as they stood side by side close to the pub wall.

'I'm filled with alcoholic benevolench,' Billy said. The tension slid out of him. Aaaah, that felt good.

Suddenly something hit him up between the legs, a ferocious pain striking hard into his groin. Unable to stop himself he bellowed in agony and fear.

There was a pause and before he could move or shake free of the pain, it struck hard and deep at him again.

'Holy shit!' roared Billy.

'It's a damned electric fence,' wailed Potu, limping backwards out of range as he realised what was attacking them. 'That bastard's electrocuted his wall!'

Inside, Michael O'Reay was polishing his perfectly clean bar tables with a spotless dustcloth. All around him the carpet was damp with fresh shampoo. He paused when he heard the bellowing from his courtyard. He smiled, then resumed his polishing. Presently, he began to whistle a lilting, Irish melody.